MAIL-ORDER BRIDES OF THE WEST:

DEBRA HOLLAND

Dedication

In loving memory of Joseph Donato Napolitano.

Thanks, "Uncle Peep" for the stories.
I'm so grateful you survived falling into the wine vat
and lived to a ripe old age.

Acknowledgments

I have many people to be thankful to for their help in writing Lina's story.

Don Napolitano, for six happy years with an Italian family. Because of you, I know red sauce runs in an Italian's blood.

To Caroline Fyffe for going with my idea to have a joint mail-order bride series. This has been so much fun!

To Elizabeth Jennings, author, expatriate living in Italy, for the help with Italian words and phrases.

To Allie K. Adams, author, Montana resident, with thanks for the hunting inspiration and research.

To my editors:
Louella Nelson, Linda Carroll-Bradd and Adela Brito

To my formatters:
Amy Atwell and Rob Preece

To my beta readers:
Hannelore Holland, Hedy Codner, Larry Codner
and Kandice Hutton

To my cousin and personal assistant:
Mindy Codner Freed.

MAIL-ORDER BRIDES OF THE WEST:

Lina

1886

SEVEN YEARS BEFORE

WILD MONTANA SKY

TAKES PLACE

Chapter One

Angelina Napolitano sat at the table in the kitchen of her employer's mansion, finishing her breakfast and reading yesterday's newspaper—an infrequent indulgence in her normally busy life. But then again, this was an unusual day. Instead of herding the three Hensley boys to keep them out of trouble, she was about to become unemployed.

Currently, her charges were having a farewell breakfast in the dining room with their parents instead of eating with her in the playroom. Biting her lip to hold back a wave of sadness, Lina forced herself to keep reading. But the words blurred until only an ad printed in bold letters stood out.

MAIL-ORDER BRIDES OF THE WEST AGENCY
SEEKS WOMEN OF GOOD REPUTATION
AND ACCOMPLISHED IN DOMESTIC SKILLS
TO TRAVEL WEST TO BECOME WIVES
OF GENTLEMEN EAGER TO WED
Character references required,
preferably from a minister or other reputable person.

The ad went on to give details about sending enquiries to a Mrs. Seymour. Her attention caught, Lina blinked away tears and read the advertisement again. Thoughts whirling, she settled back in her chair. She'd been dreading the return to her family home—one of a long row of narrow houses owned by her family members. Their crowded street overflowed with relatives—her parents, five siblings, their children, her nonna, aunts, uncles, cousins, and all their various offspring.

Her family was boisterous, warm, and nosy. As much as Lina loved them, she knew she'd never have a moment's privacy or any peace. Her mama would pester her to get married and provide her with grandchildren, as if the eleven she already had weren't enough; her aunts would send over potential suitors, including the fishmonger and garbage collector's sons; and her brothers would become fiercely protective, as if she hadn't lived on her own and provided for herself since she was eighteen. She was ready to settle down, although not with a man her relatives chose, and longed for children of her own.

Imagining that future made Lina shudder. For the last eight years, she'd worked as a nanny, living in a mansion of calm and elegance—unless, as often happened, the boys caused mischief. At first, the hush of the large chambers had been hard to become used to. But from the beginning, she loved having her own attic room instead of sharing one with two sisters. The last thing she wanted was to return to her chaotic home.

She reread the ad for mail-order brides. *Dare I travel out West? Marry a man I don't know?* The idea both thrilled and terrified her.

The clatter of pots drew her attention to the sink where Arie, the scullery maid, washed the breakfast pans. Arie was usually careful with the dishes, especially since a slip brought the wrath of Cook down on her head.

Lina looked at the girl in inquiry, an eyebrow raised.

Arie shot a guilty glance at the deep pantry, where Cook was inside tallying their supplies before she placed a grocery order. Lips pressed tight, she looked back at Lina. "I'm sorry for disturbing your reading." Leaning forward, she scrubbed an iron skillet. "It's just with all the comings and goings, the house at sixes and sevens... I can't keep my mind on my work." She sniffed. "It's not going to be the same around here. The master and mistress gone to Europe, all the boys, even little Master Jimmy, away to school, and you leaving."

Lina sent Arie a reassuring smile. "You'll have a lot less work with the family gone."

Arie lifted one thin shoulder. "Cook and Mrs. Miller will have me polishing the silver and scrubbing the basement, and..."

As she heard the litany of chores, Lina sent up a prayer of thankfulness that she didn't have to work as a housemaid in a mansion doing the often-backbreaking work of scrubbing floors, toting pails of coal to the fireplaces, fetching and carrying items up and down several flights of stairs. Once she tucked the boys in bed, her time was her own. The Hensleys allowed her to borrow books from their extensive, and mostly unused, library, so she spent many evenings reading.

While she listened to Arie, Lina stood and crossed to a cabinet, hunting for scissors in a drawer. Returning to the table, she cut out the mail-order bride advertisement. She rolled up the square of paper and tucked the ticket to a possible future into the long sleeve of her black uniform. Then she folded the newspaper and set it in the pile of trash to be burned.

A chiming sound made Lina look up to the central bell panel to see the ringing bell situated over the neatly label *nanny*. *That's me. But not for long.* With a sigh of sadness, she rose, smoothed her dress, and left the kitchen to attend her final interview with Mrs. Hensley.

With heavy steps, she climbed the stairs to the first floor and veered to the opening that led into the entryway. New steamer trunks sat on the black-and-white tiled floor. The lid of one was propped open, the top tilted back against the carved panel wall. The lace-edged sleeve of a dress trailed over the side. More trunks lined the hallway—the ones for the boys already packed with their clothes and gear for boarding school. Seeing them made her throat tighten, and Lina hurried into Mrs. Hensley's sitting room.

Her employer, wearing a blue day dress, sat at her desk going over a list. She looked up and gave Lina a frazzled smile. "I don't know why I let Mr. Hensley talk me into leaving for Europe on the same day we're sending the boys off to school."

After eight years of working for kind Mrs. Hensley, Lina was comfortable enough with her mistress to speak in a familiar manner. "Because he didn't want you to feel sadness of an empty house without your *bambinos*." Lina slipped into Italian, as she tended to do when upset. "Your babies," she corrected.

Mrs. Hensley's face relaxed. "I know. He was trying to spare me the pain of the last of my chicks flying the nest."

"Not just you, ma'am. He'll miss the boys, too."

"Our scamps." Moisture sheened Mrs. Hensley's gray eyes. She pressed her lips together, briskly reached for an envelope on the desk, and handed it to Lina. "A reference, your final pay, and a bonus for a job well done."

Lina took the envelope and swallowed hard. When she touched the paper, her fingers trembled. "Thank you, ma'am. I'm going to miss the boys, too."

"What will you do now, Angelina?"

"I'll go home for a while, but..." A sudden impulse made Lina fish out the advertisement from her sleeve and hand the scrap of paper to her employer. "I just read about this today, and I'm considering answering."

Mrs. Hensley read the ad, and her brows pulled together. "I know Margaret Seymour. The Seymours are an old St. Louis family. Mrs. Seymour is an...unusual woman. Her husband was in the army, and she traveled all over the West with him. I've heard good things about how reputable her agency is. But still—" she shook her head "—becoming a mail-order bride...it's a big risk." She handed back the ad.

Lina folded up the paper and tucked it into her sleeve.

"My suggestion is that you don't marry right away—at least not for a couple of days after the initial meeting. Make sure you like the looks of the man—that he has all his teeth, for example—and that his home and occupation are as he professed them to be. I'm sure Mrs. Seymour will be fine with you having a short waiting period."

I hadn't thought of those possibilities. Fingers clutching the envelope, Lina gave her employer a wobbly smile. "Good advice, ma'am."

Mrs. Hensley gave a small shake of her head. "If this is what you decide to do, I'll write Margaret Seymour a recommendation on your behalf."

"Thank you, ma'am." Lina's stomach tightened. Mrs. Hensley's generous offer made the possibility of becoming a mail-order bride more real. "If you could write the letter to Mrs. Seymour before you leave…so I have it just in case…"

Such a drastic step will require careful thinking.

Chapter Two

Sweetwater Springs, Montana
June 1886

The day Adam fell into the fire was the day Jonah Barrett knew he needed to find the child a mother.

Jonah hadn't left the toddler alone in the house for long, just to milk the new cow. But he emerged from the barn to hear pain-filled shrieks from his son. His stomach leapt into his throat. He had only enough presence of mind not to drop the milk pail before racing to the house and throwing open the door.

His eighteen-month-old son knelt in front of the fireplace, screaming and holding out a burned hand.

Feeling gut-kicked, Jonah performed a quick examination to make sure Adam wasn't hurt anywhere else, then he scooped the boy into his arms and rushed outside. At the pump perched above a half-barrel trough, he worked the handle and thrust Adam's hand into the cold water.

Adam squirmed and bellowed, shaking his head with each scream.

His heart racing, Jonah held his son tight, talking in a soothing voice and keeping the boy's hand in the water.

Eventually, the screams died down to whimpers, and Jonah's heartbeat calmed.

Adam looked up at him, green eyes drenched and dark eyelashes clumped. Fat tears continued to roll down his face, and he sniffled.

Jonah pressed a kiss to Adam's forehead, feeling a mixture of guilt and sorrow for the little one's injury. "I'm so sorry, baby. Pa's so very sorry. I shouldn't have left you alone." He rose and carried the boy to the icehouse dug into the side of the hill, opened the door, and ducked inside. The resin scent of the thick sawdust mounded over the blocks of ice to keep them frozen permeated the chilly air. He brushed a forearm across the top of a block to remove the layer of sawdust, yanked his handkerchief from his pocket and dropped it on a patch of ice, then set Adam's burned hand on the frozen surface.

The boy sobbed and tried to pull away.

Gritting his teeth, Jonah held him firmly, feeling like a horrible father to torture his son so. "This will make you better, little one. I promise."

Adam stopped struggling. He took shuddering breaths that shook his little frame.

After about ten minutes, Jonah judged the heat from the injury had cooled enough for the toddler to bear. He took Adam inside and closely studied the wound. The skin on the boy's palm was red and blistered—painful, to be sure, but to Jonah's relief, it didn't look as if the burn would cause serious damage to the child's hand. He gently slathered bear grease from a crock in the kitchen over the wound and tied a clean handkerchief around the hand.

Jonah boiled some willow bark tea, and, once the brew had cooled, he held the cup to the boy's lips until he'd drank a sufficient amount. Then he took Adam outside to the bench on the porch and sat.

Suddenly exhausted, he leaned his head back, stroking the child's soft, dark hair and rubbing his back. The motion soothed them both, and soon Adam drifted into sleep.

For the first time since the accident, Jonah had a chance to think about what had happened. He'd been doing his chores around the farm. The child had already had some close calls when Jonah's back was turned—once the cow almost kicked him. So he'd left Adam in the house by himself, thinking that would be safer. He'd certainly told the boy often enough to mind the stove and the fireplace, and had thought Adam understood.

The pain and helplessness from the last frustrating weeks since his wife Koko's death birthing their stillborn daughter threatened to overwhelm him. *What am I going to do?*

He couldn't take an active toddler along while doing chores. Both the work and the boy suffered. Adam had outgrown his papoose, so Jonah couldn't carry him on his back, and he was afraid to tie him up, lest he become tangled in the rope.

Koko's parents would help, but they were several days' travel away. He had lost his wife and daughter and couldn't abide the idea of losing Adam too, even if he could visit his son from time to time.

Thinking of her family made more guilt twist his guts.

When I return to the Blackfoot for a visit with Adam, should I marry another squaw and bring her back with me? The idea held appeal, mostly because that act would be easier than courting a white woman. And a woman who looked like Adam's mother might be comforting for the child.

But what would be easy for Jonah would ultimately be difficult for them both. Many of the townsfolk had shunned him after he'd brought back an Indian wife from the reservation. He hadn't considered that reaction when he'd become captivated by a girl racing her horse, her long dark hair streaming behind her, and had married her. Koko's name meant *black*, for her thick fall of hair.

All in all, the attitude of the citizens of Sweetwater Springs about his marriage hadn't bothered him too much. As the son of the town drunk, Jonah had suffered enough taunts and jeers over the years—hence his decision to choose a squaw for a wife because none of the available women in town would give him the time of day, much less marry him.

But when they had their first baby, everything changed. Jonah loved Adam with a deep fierceness he'd never thought possible. Knowing the boy was a half-breed, would be thought of and treated as a second-class citizen—no, worse than a second-class citizen—had weighed on his mind.

The prejudices of the town helped him decide. Another Indian wife, no matter how convenient now, would ultimately make their lives more difficult.

But to choose a white wife...even if he could find a decent woman who'd take him, would she love Adam or just tolerate the boy? Or worse...would she mistreat him when Jonah's back was turned—when he couldn't protect him?

But I'm not protecting him now. Familiar guilt surged through him, intensified by today's accident. As he rocked, Jonah sorted through the women he knew. Not that he knew many, due to rarely visiting town and not socializing with anyone except for an occasional drink with Seth Flanigan.

Thinking of his friend gave Jonah an idea. Seth had recently married a mail-order bride. A pretty woman from what he'd observed when he'd run into the couple in town. He hadn't known about Trudy Flanigan being a mail-order bride until a few weeks later; he'd heard the gossip when he'd taken his gelding to the blacksmith shop to be shod.

That decided him. When Adam woke up, he and the boy would ride over to the Flanigan farm to consult with the couple about the possibility of a mail-order bride.

☙

In the front yard of Seth's farm, Jonah reined in his horse, astonished at the changes in the place since he'd last visited. Both he and Adam, sitting tucked in front of him, stared around with interest.

The house had a new coat of whitewash. Instead of hard-packed dirt sprouting spindly weeds here and there, a flagstone path led down a green lawn. Colorful flowers bloomed in beds edging the grass and in front of the porch. Two halves of a wooden barrel, not unlike the one Jonah used for a water trough, were sunk into each side of the walkway. More flowers bloomed within them. A couple of black chickens pecked on the lawn.

Jonah hadn't realized how much the Flanigan spread had gotten run-down in recent years until he saw it now. With a sinking heart, he realized his house probably looked just as bad. Trudy had remained with Seth after she'd seen his home, but by then they were already married. Seth knew about the state of Jonah's property. Therefore, Trudy would too. Would she disapprove and not want another woman coming out to a similarly neglected home?

And take on the added responsibility of a child not her own. He glanced down at Adam's silky black hair. *And one who is a half-breed.*

Before Jonah could decide where to head his horse, toward the house or the barn, he spotted a blond woman stepping out on the porch. He took off his hat so Trudy Flanigan could see who he was. "Afternoon, Miz Flanigan."

Her face lit with a smile, and she waved. "Ride on up here, Mr. Barrett. You can hitch your horse to the porch rail."

Jonah nudged his mount forward until he reached the watering trough situated near the front porch.

Mrs. Flanigan trotted down the steps and hurried over. "I guess Seth will have to make a hitching rail at the edge of the lawn. You're the first visitor we've had since we set out the grass, and we didn't think about what to do with people's horses." She glanced at his son. "I'm so glad you brought Adam." Her gaze sharpened. "What happened to his hand?"

"He burned himself."

"Oh, the poor little tyke." She held up her arms. "Will you come to me, Adam?"

"Probably not, ma'am. He's not used to strangers."

Sure enough, the boy shrank back against Jonah's middle.

"Sorry about that, ma'am."

"Please call me Trudy."

"Only if you'll call me Jonah." With his free hand, he rubbed

Adam's back. "Come on, son. Let me put you down." He plucked the boy from the saddle and lifted him into Trudy's arms.

Adam puckered his face about to wail.

Jonah quickly dismounted, looped the reins around the rail, and took back his son, jiggling him a little. "There, there, now. It's all right."

"I've just taken oatmeal cookies out of the oven. Come in and let me get you two something to eat. Then I'll go hunt up Seth. I think he's in the barn."

"How 'bout you let me go find him? I'm familiar with your barn."

"Yes, of course. You know the way. Would you like tea, milk, or water to go with your cookies?"

"We can try milk with Adam. I only bought a cow since his ma died, and he's not too sure about the taste of milk yet. But I like it just fine."

With a gentle touch, she stroked a finger on Adam's cheek. "I don't blame him. He's had a lot of changes thrust on him, poor little boy."

A surge of hope lifted Jonah's spirits somewhat. Maybe Trudy had been thinking along the same lines as he had. That would make broaching the topic of a mail-order bride easier.

At that moment, Seth came out of the barn, carrying a shovel.

Trudy called his name.

Seth looked up and spotted Jonah. He waved and propped the shovel against the side of the barn before striding over to them.

Seth looks good and healthy. His friend had always been on the thin side. Now he'd put on a few pounds, probably due to Trudy's cooking. Jonah thought of the loose waistband in his pants. He, too, could stand to put on more weight.

"Jonah!" Wearing a big grin, Seth slapped his shoulder. "Hello, little shaver." He rubbed Adam's head. To Jonah he said, "You haven't been here for I don't know how long. Before you were married." His smile dimmed for a second, but he caught himself and patted Jonah's shoulder again. "It's good to see you. Please come in and make yourself at home." He gestured toward the house.

"Yes, do." Trudy hurried up the stairs ahead of them.

Carrying Adam, Jonah followed Trudy into the Flanigan home, where he inhaled the mouth-watering smell of oatmeal cookies. The scent took him back to his childhood, to his mother laughing and smacking his hand when he tried to swipe a hot one just out of the oven. With a feeling of grief, he recalled how once they'd cooled, she'd poured out a fresh glass of milk and had let him eat two. The sweet treat had filled his stomach, and Jonah remembered her fond look as he ate. Not long after, she'd died in childbirth, and he hadn't had an oatmeal cookie since.

Jonah swallowed down old grief and looked around. The kitchen took up most of the left side of the room, and the sitting area was on the right.

His first impression was of furniture. The kitchen had a table covered with a red-checked cloth, the stove, dry sink, pie safe, buffet holding dishes, built-in cupboards and open shelving. A crystal vase held wildflowers.

Across the room a bookshelf stuffed with volumes stood against the wall. A settee and two wingback chairs, with small marble-topped tables in between, framed the fireplace. Oil lamps stood on the tables, the glass chimneys sparkling in the sun. With guilt, he thought of the soot-smudged single lamp he had at home. He hadn't cleaned the chimney for a few days. One of the many little chores he never had time for.

Trudy bustled over to a wire rack on top of the stove. She took a spatula and deftly scooped the cookies onto a white platter, which she placed on the table.

Seth motioned Jonah to the table.

Jonah pulled out a chair and sat, holding Adam on his knee. He leaned forward to see the child's face.

Adam stared at Seth with big eyes.

Trudy brought over more plates and a glass of milk, setting a plate in front of the two men and one of the empty chairs. She handed Jonah the glass of milk. "See how he likes this. But give him a bite of a cookie first. Milk always tastes better after something sweet."

Jonah set the glass on the table and reached for a cookie, breaking off a piece and handing it to Adam. Then he popped a section in his own mouth to show his son how good it was. "Mmmm."

The boy brought the cookie to his mouth and began to eat. Obviously liking the taste, he quickly gobbled up the rest and, with his uninjured hand, reached for another.

For the first time since Adam's accident, Jonah felt the raw edges of his guilt smooth away. He held the glass so the boy could take a few gulps of milk, which he seemed to like.

Trudy brought more glasses and poured milk for all of them before taking a seat. "I'm glad Adam likes my baking."

Seth swallowed his own bite. "That's because everything you make is a treat to eat, Trudy."

Trudy's eyes sparkled at the compliment.

Jonah ran a hand over his son's head. "Adam's been off his feed lately. Hard to get him interested in anything I make. So I'm glad to see him eating."

A pleased expression made Trudy's blue eyes glow. "I'll send some cookies home with you," she promised. "Now, Jonah. Please tell us how you've been getting along these months?"

While Jonah fed Adam small bites of cookies, he relayed the story of what had happened that morning.

Trudy placed a hand on her chest. "How frightening for you both."

Jonah couldn't bear to see the sympathy in her eyes. He looked down at the table. "Adam needs a mother. But I want someone who will genuinely care for him."

"I have something I've been wanting to discuss with you, Mr..., ah Jonah." Trudy leaned forward. "A possible solution for your circumstances."

"That bridal agency you came from?"

"You read my mind."

"Do you know anyone there who'd fit the bill?"

Trudy wrinkled her forehead. "But what about yourself, Jonah? What do you want in a wife besides a good mother to Adam?"

"I think someone who'd care for the boy—not mind him being a half-breed—is as good as I can ask for."

With a shake of his head, Seth reached for another cookie. "I think you should think on this." He sent a fond glance at his wife. "I was pretty specific about the kind of woman I wanted, and Mrs. Seymour delivered that and even more than I could have dreamed in a wife."

A blush crept in to Trudy's cheeks, making her look adorable.

Should I ask for a pretty wife? Jonah gave an inward shake of his head. *I'll take the woman who is given me as long as she makes Adam happy.* "A good mother will suit me just fine."

Trudy wrinkled her nose. "I wish I knew you better, so I could be sure to recommend the best candidate. Remember, I've been gone from the agency for a month. But I knew Heather, Lina, Darcy, Kathryn, and Bertha. All lovely women." Trudy smiled, the look in her eyes one of reminiscing. "It's surprising really, how close we became in a short time—with one notable exception who had an unpleasant personality. We were not normally the kind of women who probably would have become dear friends given our differing social class, level of education, and even religion. But our shared fear and excitement, the knowledge of the common risks we were about to undertake…"

Seth dropped his hand over his wife's and gave her a quick squeeze. "I'm glad you were brave enough."

Trudy sent him a look of love before turning back to Jonah. "By this time, there may even be some new brides. But the woman I'm thinking about is Lina Napolitano. She loves children, looks forward to being a mother, and also wants to be a stepmother. She's worked as a nanny to three rambunctious boys who adored her, but now they're old enough to go to school. Lina loves to cook and introduced us to Italian food. Have you had pasta and red sauce, Jonah?"

He shook his head.

"Then you're in for a treat."

"If she's Italian…" He pondered the implications. "Dark hair and eyes? Olive skin?"

"Yes. She has a voluptuous figure. And corkscrew curly hair." Adam squirmed to get down.

Trudy rose. "Let me get him something to keep him occupied, although perhaps he'll be noisy." She gathered a wooden spoon, a pot, and a tin pan, and placed them on the floor near Adam.

The boy picked up the wooden spoon and began to tap the floor.

Trudy guided him to thump on the pot and the pan before standing and resuming her seat.

Jonah repressed a sigh. "I've sometimes thought Adam might be better off when he grows up by leaving Sweetwater Springs…" Just the idea made his gut twist, and Jonah brushed a hand over his son's head. "Somewhere where he wouldn't be known as a half-breed. Where he wouldn't suffer from…" He shrugged, not able to put into words the critical glances, cold shoulders and turned backs, the jeers, having to defend himself far too often with his fists, which Adam would have to endure in the town of his birth. "He could pass himself off as Italian."

Silence followed his rather impassioned speech.

Trudy, a look of dismay on her face, glanced at Seth. "Will it really be that bad for him?"

Seth glanced at Adam. His jaw tightened. "It could be. From some people."

"But not from us," Trudy said with a fierce light in her eyes. Her hand clenched her glass so hard the knuckles whitened. "And I refuse to believe the Nortons and the Camerons and the Carters would lend themselves to such low behavior."

"Perhaps not," Jonah said quietly, running a finger around the top of his glass. "But I don't cross the paths of those people. I've never spoken to the Carters. Nodded. Tipped my hat to Mrs. Carter, but that's about it."

"I never did have much truck with them either." Seth grinned at his wife. "Then my mail-order bride arrived on the train and turned my life upside down by charming everyone she met and making acquaintances for us."

Trudy gave him a slight shake of her head, the pink returning to her cheeks.

Jonah couldn't even let himself dream of an agreeable match like the Flanigans had made. "I'd settle for a mail-order bride taking my upside down life and making it right side up."

"We want that for you as well," Seth said.

Trudy stood, walked over to one of the round tables, then returned with a portable desk and set it on the table. She lifted the lid and took out a piece of stationary, an inkwell, and a pen. "Might as well write your letter to Mrs. Seymour. While you work on yours, I can write one to Lina and encourage her to accept you. Then you can ride to town and ask Reverend Norton for a reference."

Jonah's heart sank, and he slumped back in his chair. "Reverend Norton wouldn't write me a reference."

"Reverend Norton? Why ever not?"

"Thing is, I haven't set foot in a church in years," Jonah said, feeling shame clamp his insides to admit the truth. "Not since I was eight. Once my mother died, my father refused to go to church. He was pretty angry at God."

"But what about you, Jonah?" Trudy said softly. "You're an adult. Why aren't you going to church?"

"I didn't have the habit of it, I guess. Maybe some of Pa's anger seeped into me." He'd never thought of that before— would have to ponder the idea further.

"Not even when you married?"

"We married by the Blackfoot traditions."

Eyebrows raised, Trudy glanced at Adam.

"I know what you're thinking…that Adam is an *illegitimate* half-breed." Jonah tried to keep the bitterness out of his voice. Maybe he had become too much like his father. "Not long after I brought Koko home, Reverend and Mrs. Norton showed up unannounced. Without further ado, he married us proper. I have the paper to prove it."

Trudy's expression cleared. "If you are to wed one of my friends, Jonah, you must start attending service. Lina's Catholic. Would you be willing to convert?"

Father Fredrick only holds services once a month. I think I can agree to that. He nodded.

"Good." She drummed the fingers of one hand on the table. "But that doesn't take care of your reference."

Seth swallowed the last of his milk and set down the empty glass. "Reverend Norton doesn't need to send a reference, my dear. I remember the wording in that advertisement very well. Mrs. Seymour asked for references from the minister *or another reputable person.* I'm sure she'll consider you reputable." His gray eyes lit with laughter. "Didn't you need to have a good reputation to even qualify as one of her mail-order brides?"

Trudy wrinkled her nose at Seth. "You're right." She looked at Jonah. "Of course, I can write Mrs. Seymour a reference on your behalf."

"Mrs. Seymour had another stipulation that I should warn you about, Jonah," Seth said in a drawl. "She requires the man to refrain from attempting marital relations for at least a month in order to give the woman time to adjust to her new situation. Course, the woman can always jump the gun if she chooses." He slanted a knowing grin at his wife.

There will be no problem with that. He hadn't felt those kinds of feelings since Koko died. Besides, his needs didn't matter. Adam's did.

Although Trudy blushed, she ignored Seth, seemingly intent on giving Jonah a piece of stationary and taking one for herself. "This is so exciting. I can't wait until Lina arrives here. She's going to fall *so* in love with Adam."

That was exactly what Jonah wanted, so why did he suddenly wish for more—love for himself as well? He squashed the feeling, picked up the pen, dipped the tip in the inkwell, and began to write.

Dear Mrs. Seymour,

On the advice of Mrs. Seth Flanigan, I am writing to your agency to send for a bride. You've requested information on my house and occupation. I'm a hunter and I farm land in a forested valley outside of Sweetwater Springs, Montana. My home is small and made of logs, but it is also sturdy and well protected against the bitter winters. I was educated for several years at the local school, but then my father, the son of a schoolteacher, took over my lessons.

He cut a glance at Trudy. "Your letter will fill in the details about me? I feel uncomfortable describing myself."

"Just be honest about your circumstances, Jonah. I'll tell Mrs. Seymour and Lina the rest."

I will be blunt about my situation because I have no desire to mislead any woman. Indeed, I need you (for my young son Adam's sake) to find a match who will be the most compatible for his well-being.

My deceased wife was an Indian, and thus my almost two-year-old son is a half-breed. My new wife must be able to accept him and also accept the fact that we will keep ties to his mother's family. I swore this when I wed her, and on this issue, I will not change my mind.

He looked at Trudy. "Will contact with Koko's Indian family frighten Lina?"

Trudy pursed her lips, thinking. "I'm sure at first she will be disconcerted, as any woman would be. But if you've reassured her beforehand...explained any customs Lina needs to know about so she can extend the proper hospitality..."

He gave her a tight smile. "Politeness and good food will, as they do in most situations, go a long way to making our guests comfortable." He dipped the pen in the ink and began the disclosure he was most reticent to make.

Visits from the Black foot might not be the worst of her social challenges. I must also warn you that some of the townsfolk look down on me and Adam, and we are not always treated well. Perhaps that situation will change with the arrival of a bride from St. Louis, and the friendship of the Flanigans will certainly help. I just want my wife to be prepared for those possibilities.

I have given a lot of thought to the boy's future. Far too many half-breeds live unhappy lives, belonging to neither race. Within my bond of keeping my promise to his mother, and if Adam so desires, I want him to be able to disappear into the white man's world. If we visit, I'd like my bride to have the kind of family who would welcome him.

But my wife should know that I have no family of my own, and she will have no in-laws either to turn to for support or to disturb her peace with their demands.

Although I sound firm and perhaps like a domestic tyrant, I assure you I am no such man. I am of even temperament, quiet, and contemplative, and if truth be told, even a little melancholy. My firmness in this letter is to prevent a match that would ill suit my wife and me. For if she is uncomfortable with my son's Indian heritage, we all will be made unhappy.

Sincerely,

Jonah Barrett

He blew on the ink of the last few sentences to dry the words, then handed the letter to Trudy. "Tell me what you think?"

Her eyes scanned the page. "You write quite eloquently."

"Not bad for only two years of schooling," Jonah said in a wry tone.

"I didn't mean that." Trudy's soft voice had a sharp edge. "I think it's important to write with a literate hand when you are courting a potential bride. I know Lina likes to read, but I have not seen a sample of her writing."

Jonah felt ashamed of his ill-humor. Trudy Flanigan was only trying to help.

"Forgive me, Trudy, I didn't mean to offend."

"You didn't…" She cast an uncertain glance at her husband. "It's just that I don't like to hear you speaking poorly of yourself, much less assume I'd think of you in such ways." Her tone lightened. "If you're not careful, I'll think you're lumping me in with the Cobbs."

"No, no, never." Jonah said. "The Cobbs have a category all their own." He made sure the ink was dry, folded the paper, and handed the letter to Trudy. "I'm placing an order for a mother for Adam."

Chapter Three

St. Louis
Five Days Later

Lina stood at the stove in the kitchen of the Victorian mansion housing the Mail-Order Brides of the West Agency, teaching the other women how to make her nonna's soup. After living together for a month, she and several of the potential brides had grown close, and a cooking lesson involved a lot of laughter, especially for a dish that didn't involve a recipe. She suggested the ladies create Nonna's soup with whatever was available in the kitchen.

She'd filled the huge enamel pot brought from her parents' home in the Italian part of St. Louis with water and dropped in a chicken carcass left over from luncheon to boil. She measured out the Italian spices, placing the proper amount in minute piles on a platter. Across from the little mounds of herbs, she placed the bottle or bag the spice had come from. "Rosemary, thyme, basil, parsley, and oregano," Lina told them as she pointed at each.

She added two garlic cloves to the end of the platter. "Garlic is essential in Italian cooking and easy to grow in your kitchen garden. It's also very healthy for you. But the flavor is strong and not suitable for every palate. Experiment. Discover what your future spouse or family likes and adjust your recipe accordingly."

"Do you use all of them at once?" Heather asked, her beautiful green eyes full of interest.

"I won't add all these spices to the soup today. Depending on my mood and what was available to add to the pot, I will use a different combination. But I want you all to see the possibilities and the amounts to use. Just telling you a pinch of oregano won't be much help when you have to make your own soup."

While she worked, Lina set the other brides to chopping up vegetables. She'd given shrewish Prudence the onions, figuring if the woman was busy wiping her eyes from the onion fumes, she wouldn't have a chance to annoy anyone else. Lina glanced around the kitchen, checking on everyone, feeling like a general assessing her troops.

Kathryn stood at the sink peeling potatoes. Her long, graceful fingers, so proficient on the piano keys, fumbled with the spuds. Even as Lina glanced in her direction, the potato popped out of Kathryn's hand and slid across the sink. The woman gave an exclamation of annoyance and picked it up. She determinedly hacked away, not having learned the long gliding strokes that were the most efficient way to shave off the skin.

Lina hid her smile, picked up an egg, and cracked it into a bowl.

Darcy, tall enough to lean over Lina, dropped a handful of chopped carrots into the pot. "I wonder how long Mrs. Seymour will take to read through that stack of mail on her desk." For once, Darcy's well-modulated voice betrayed a hint of eagerness.

Lina had often wondered if her friend ever raised her voice. She imagined Darcy's family sitting around the dinner table, all conversing in the same proper tones, and contrasted the scene with her own family—many speaking at the same time, interrupting, talking over each other, and often switching back and forth between English and Italian.

On the other side of the kitchen, Dona the cook helped

plump, blond Bertha make bread. Dona was a big-framed woman who towered over the rest of them. She kneaded dough with sturdy strokes while Bertha cut a pattern with a knife on the top of a loaf she was about to place into the oven. Bertha baked the best bread of all of them and had no need for Lina's cooking lesson. When Darcy mentioned the letters, she looked up, a beaming smile on her broad face. "Maybe Mrs. Seymour will have matches for all of us."

Prudence sniffed and wiped her sleeve across her eyes. "She should. Mrs. Seymour's been visiting Evie Davenport. I can't imagine why she'd want to. Evie was a servant here."

"Evie *Holcomb*, Prudence." Lina couldn't resist the reminder that sweet Evie, servant girl or not, had married before all of them.

Prudence ignored her and turned her gaze to the others. "Mrs. Seymour has been gone for two weeks. That's wasted time as far as I'm concerned. I've been here entirely too long. It's not at *all* what I expected."

Lina exchanged glances with Heather, her best friend at the agency.

The dark-haired girl's lips quivered with amusement, and her green eyes danced. A few days earlier, Prudence had let slip about a prior match Mrs. Seymour had arranged for her.

"Well, you did have a chance, Prudence," Heather said. "The offer that came before the rest of us arrived at the agency. You turned him down."

"Huh!" Lips pursed in disapproval, Prudence sniffed back onion-tears and raised her chin. Somehow the redness in her eyes took the usual arrogance out of the gesture. "I could do better than *that man*."

Heather bent close to Lina's ear. "*That man* had a lucky escape," she whispered.

Lina suppressed a giggle. She suspected Mrs. Seymour had caught on to Prudence's ways and was having to work hard to find a fit for the disagreeable woman—probably someone just as unpleasant—a couple who'd be miserable no matter who they married, so it might as well be to each other.

As the brides chattered about potential matches—a favorite topic, made more interesting today by their speculation about the offers in that stack of letters—Lina's thoughts drifted to the future—one that might be only a few days away. She imagined acquiring a family who desperately needed her. She'd become a mother, perhaps with several adoring step-children. She could almost see her new daughter's curls and the look of mischief on one of her son's faces. The other boy was shy, she imagined, and she had to coax him to come close, but for that very reason perhaps she loved him best. Their father was a shadowy figure, looking upon her with approval, which soon turned to adoration. Soon she added a dark-haired baby in her arms to that picture. *My family.* She held the dream close to her heart and hoped Mrs. Seymour finally had a match for her.

❦

The next morning before breakfast, when Lina reached the bottom of the staircase, pulling on her gardening gloves on her way to cut some roses for the table, she found Mrs. Seymour waiting. Her heart began to pound.

The matron wore one of her military style dresses in a navy-blue that matched her eyes. "Ah, Lina, my dear. I was just setting out to look for you. I have some exciting news to share. Please come into my office."

Suddenly, Lina's breath shortened. *Does she have a match for me?* Removing her gloves, Lina followed in Mrs. Seymour's wake. They walked across the entry, through the double parlor, and into the office. Lina hadn't been in the room since her first interview, but she loved the round space housed in the Victorian's turret, with sunlight streaming through the large lace-covered windows.

Mrs. Seymour waved her to a seat in front of her desk and took her place behind it. She picked up a letter, leaned forward, and handed her the folded paper. "This is for you from Trudy

Flanigan. It came with a proposal from a prospective husband she's recommending for you."

Trudy? Setting her gloves in her lap, Lina took the letter. *How odd.* She unfolded the sheet of paper. Her fingers trembled with anticipation. She began to read.

Dear Lina,

I hope this letter finds you well. I'm writing to tell you that I've found you a match! I also wanted to let you know I have encouraged your prospective husband, Jonah Barrett, to apply to Mrs. Seymour for your hand in marriage and have enclosed my recommendation to the matron with this letter.

My husband Seth has been friends with Mr. Barrett since childhood, when they both were raised under unhappy circumstances. (I will let Mr. Barrett himself tell you of his boyhood, for I feel it's not my place to do so.) Recently, his Indian wife died in childbirth, and their second baby as well—a heartbreaking situation.

Mr. Barrett has a son, Adam, who is almost two—the most adorable boy you've ever seen. I'm quite in love with him! The child has his father's green eyes and his mother's dark hair and golden skin, but he's not as dark-complexioned as the Indians I've seen around here. In fact, he looks like he could be your own, except that his hair is straight instead of curly.

Mr. Barrett approached me about finding a mail-order bride because he's been having trouble managing his farm chores while caring for a toddler. I immediately thought of you because I know you want a man with children. Also with your years of working as a nanny, you already have the necessary skills to benefit this child.

I have not seen Mr. Barrett's home, but my dearest Seth has. He says the farm is small but well tended and surrounded by forest. The house is built of logs and is about the size of ours, with a main room that includes the kitchen and one bedroom. There is also a loft.

According to Seth, the house is situated so the front porch faces the mountains. I envy Mr. Barrett the majestic vista. Oh, Lina, the beauty of Montana fills my soul! Soon I hope to have a second porch on our home that will face the mountains, and I can look at them to my heart's fulfillment. But in the meantime, I must content myself with a view of farmland and the distant forests.

Seth also says Mr. Barrett's place needs work. But so too did my husband's bachelor home. Although we've worked very hard to fix it up, I've taken joy in making the house and yard as beautiful as my skill, Seth's strength, and our means allow. I'm sure you will take a similar pleasure in setting to rights the Barrett household.

As for Mr. Barrett, prior to his visiting our farm to ask for help, I'd only briefly met him once before. But I can tell you that he appears to genuinely care for Adam. His only spoken wish is for a mother who will be good to the boy. Seth tells me that Jonah is a loyal friend and a kind man. My husband says when they were young, "Jonah had a smile that would charm us out of whatever trouble we were in from the mischief the two of us caused." But I only saw his sad green eyes—the color put me in mind of a glass bottle—and once caught a glimpse of a partial smile. As far as I could tell, he has all his teeth and is a handsome man. He wears his blond hair to the shoulders, but he currently has a bushy beard, so it's hard to know the true shape of his chin. Maybe I can coax him to shave or at least trim his beard before your arrival—then it will be up to you to mold him to your preference.

See, I'm counting on you already, Lina. I find both father and son tug at my heartstrings, and if any woman can bring joy to their faces, it's you.

Perhaps I can further entice you by saying I have found Sweetwater Springs to be a welcoming community and have quickly made lovely friends who've been kind and generous. (The shopkeeper is an exception. But after all, this isn't a utopia but a normal small town.)

Unlike me, when you arrive, you'll have a friend to welcome you and be present at your wedding. Although the Barrett farm is not near ours, we can see each other in town and at social activities. Perhaps, also, we can arrange for visits from time to time.

Jonah says he is willing to convert to Catholicism for your sake, dear Lina. Perhaps once he's wed, you can get him to attend mass with you.

I'm too impatient to wait for a letter in return. Please send a telegraph. I hope, my dear friend, to start planning your wedding.

Sincerely,
Trudy Flanigan

Lina let out a breath she hadn't realized she'd been holding. Trudy's letter did indeed paint an enticing picture. She looked up at Mrs. Seymour. "Did you read this?"

"No. It was addressed to you. Would you like to read Mr. Barrett's letter, and then we can discuss whether this match interests you? I must give this warning: You may face difficulties on one or two fronts. But every match has its challenges."

"We'll trade." Intrigued and keenly anxious, Lina handed over Trudy's letter and accepted Mr. Barrett's. She felt inclined to accept the match just on Trudy's words alone, and hoped what the potential groom had to say would sway her decision in a positive manner.

Lina read each line with care, lingering over Mr. Barrett's concern for his son and especially his admission of being somewhat melancholy. This, indeed, was a small family who needed her. But the reaction of the townsfolk, dealing with Indians...the very idea sounded frightening, bringing to mind the lurid stories she'd read in her brothers' dime novels. *Don't be ridiculous. If there were real dangers from Indians, Trudy would have warned me.*

She reread the letter, admiring his bold script. Finishing, she sat back in her chair. Lina could see what Trudy meant when she mentioned the father and son tugging at her heartstrings. She, too, felt the same pull toward them. She also liked Mr. Barrett's forthrightness, his protectiveness of his child, and his loyalty to the promise he made to his wife. *All good qualities in a husband.* She met the matron's gaze. "I'm very interested in Mr. Barrett."

Mrs. Seymour let out a sigh. "Having Trudy vouch for this groom, being able to describe his appearance and his circumstances...for the man to be old friends with Trudy's husband... Why it takes much of the risk out of a mail-order marriage. There are not so many unknowns."

"You're right," Lina said. "I feel excited, and of course I'm nervous. But I'm not having the kinds of fears I did before—what if he turns out to be bald, fat, and have three other wives, or whatever terrifying possibilities my brain would dream up."

With a short nod, Mrs. Seymour smiled. "I don't blame you. I always worry about the matches I make because when selecting suitable men, I must rely on the honesty of strangers. What if they are lying?"

"That must be a heavy burden for you."

"It is. I think my screening process allows for as great a potential for compatibility as can be expected in a blind arrangement. But still, marriage is a life-long commitment. When a match works—like Trudy's or Evelyn's have..." The matron placed her hand over her heart. "I feel such relief. Such satisfaction." She dropped her hand. "Please don't share those sentiments with the other brides, Lina. No sense making them even more frightened about an unknown husband than they already are."

"Of course not."

"Now," Mrs. Seymour said in a brisk tone. "Let's discuss Mr. Barrett. I can tell you from my experience living in the west—especially being among soldiers who often had to fight the Indians who hated them—his concerns about his son are, unfortunately, all too real. Too bad the man didn't consider that before he wed a squaw." She gave a dismissive wave. "Well, what's done is done."

Although she kept her expression pleasant, Lina fired up inside at the matron's statements. In that instant, she *knew* she wanted to be Adam's mother, to love him and shield him as much as possible from the cruel slings and arrows of the world. She wanted to raise Mr. Barrett's low spirits and banish the melancholy he wrote of. She vowed to be the best wife and mother possible. And with Trudy as a friend, surely forging congenial relationships with the townsfolk wouldn't be too difficult. "I accept Mr. Barrett's proposal," she said in a firm tone.

"Wonderful!" Mrs. Seymour gave her a pleased smile. "I'll send a telegram to Trudy and ask her to pass the news to Mr. Barrett." The matron handed several pieces of stationary and two envelopes across the desk. "After breakfast, write to Trudy and Mr. Barrett. We can send off the letters in the afternoon mail. I know you'd like to spend some time with your family before you leave, so shall we say you'll depart on the seventeenth?"

"That sounds perfect." With a shiver of excitement, Lina realized that soon she would be a wife and mother.

Chapter Four

With a flurry of morning greetings, the six potential brides took their accustomed places around the large mahogany dining room table for breakfast. Although bursting to tell Heather her news, Lina hadn't had an opportunity to speak privately with her friend. As soon as she'd left Mrs. Seymour's office, she'd found the other brides gathered for the meal. But anticipation buzzed through her, and she had to school her expression to not give away her excitement.

The aroma of blueberry muffins, toast, and bacon made Lina realize how hungry she was. A snowy cloth swept down the length of the table and two crystal vases of yellow roses, picked and arranged by Kathryn, made colorful bouquets in the middle. The new maid, Juniper, had brought word for them to start without waiting for Mrs. Seymour.

Early in their stay, each woman had claimed "her" spot. Even after Megan and Trudy left, the brides hadn't closed up the spaces—both because it would have felt strange and also because doing so, at least on one side of the table, would have moved Lina next to Prudence. She'd just as soon keep her distance from the unpleasant woman. She might receive a jab with a fork as easily as Prudence stabbed with her tongue.

This morning, Lina and Heather sat side-by-side and across

the table from Darcy and Kathryn. Megan's former chair next to Kathryn remained empty, and Bertha sat by herself near the foot, placidly buttering a muffin.

Lina had just taken a mouthful of fried egg, when Mrs. Seymour swept into the room.

"Good morning, my dears," the matron said in a cheerful tone. "I trust you all slept well." She took a seat, accepted a platter of bacon from Juniper, and served herself two strips. "I just opened a lovely letter from Megan. She sends her regards to you all. She likes her new home in Wyoming and is very happy with her husband, whom she says would fit right in with her family." Her brows drew into a wrinkle. "Although, I'm not sure what she means."

Lina laughed. "Megan told us that from her groom's description of himself, with his red hair he might look like her brother. I guess she was right."

Across the table, Kathryn giggled. Her brown eyes lit up. "That's right, she did."

Mrs. Seymour waited until the women stopped their chatter. "And I also received an update from Mary Morgan, whom you knew, Prudence. I believe she recommended my agency to you. Anyway, Mary writes to tell me that she is expecting a baby."

Lina glanced at Prudence and was surprised to see a sour expression pinch her face. *You'd think if Mary was a friend, Prudence would be pleased at the news.*

Mrs. Seymour buttered a slice of toast. "I am still going through my mail and will hopefully have more good news later. In the meantime, I believe two of you ladies have announcements to make."

Gasps and *oohs* went around the room, and glances flicked like bees among flowers.

"Lina," Mrs. Seymour urged. "You go first."

Lina sent Heather an apologetic glance. "I just found out right before breakfast," she told her friend. She looked around the table, seeing everyone's expectant expressions. "This morning I accepted a match with Jonah Barrett. He lives in

Sweetwater Springs, Montana, and our Trudy Bauer, now Flanigan, recommended us to each other. He has a young son named Adam, and you all know that I wanted a man with children. I'm halfway in love with little Adam already!"

Heather reached out and gave Lina's hand a squeeze.

Katherine clapped. "Wonderful! You'll get to live in the same town as Trudy. Tell us about Mr. Barrett. Does Trudy say he's handsome?"

"Indeed she does." Lina filled them in on the details. When she finished, she let out a long breath and placed a hand on her stomach, feeling the flutter of excitement. "The match is so new that I can't quite believe it yet. I'm sort of jumpy. I guess the decision will take a while to settle in my mind."

Mrs. Seymour bestowed an understanding smile on Lina. "That jumpy feeling is common. You'll find that once you accept a man, everything happens so fast… You might not get used to your new life for months." She glanced at Heather and dipped her chin. "Now for our next announcement. Last night, I asked Heather not to say anything about her match until she made her decision, which she just gave me this morning."

"You, too?" Lina looked at Heather in shock.

"Sorry," her friend mouthed before turning to the others. "I've accepted Hayden Klinkner, who lives in Y Knot, Montana Territory, Evie Davenport…Evie Holcomb lives there, too."

Mrs. Seymour beamed in approval. "I met Heather's man when I visited. He comes from a fine family. I believe a strong personality like Heather's will be just what Mr. Klinkner needs."

Kathryn clamored for details.

Over the past weeks, Heather hadn't seemed excited about the idea of marriage. Lina had the impression she was doing her duty by leaving St. Louis—one less mouth to feed in her overcrowded family. But now as Heather told what she knew about Mr. Klinkner, her friend sounded more animated than Lina had ever heard.

Although she listened carefully, Lina could barely finish her breakfast. She was too nervous about her own match *and* about Heather's to eat any more.

Before this, she hadn't paid much attention to where Trudy and Evie were actually living. Maybe the two towns weren't very far apart, and she and Heather would be able to visit from time to time. Lina made a mental note to ask Mrs. Seymour if she had a map of Montana.

But even as she fantasized about Heather coming to Sweetwater Springs and meeting Jonah and Adam, she knew that their lives would probably grow apart. They might never see each other again, and that thought pinched her heart.

Not until after breakfast did Lina and Heather, both excused from cleaning up after the meal, have a chance to go to their attic dormitory and talk. They sat on Trudy's old bed and shared the men's letters, each reading about the others' prospective match. Afterward, Heather read Trudy's. They discussed their weddings and planned what to wear for the ceremony.

With obvious reluctance, Heather brought an end to their discussion. "If I'm leaving tomorrow, I need to pack and go home for a final..." Her voice caught, and she took a steadying breath. "Visit."

So soon. A lump formed in Lina's throat. She reached out, took Heather's hand, and squeezed. "I know how hard it will be leaving them, especially Melba," she said, referring to Heather's little sister who had a lingering illness.

Tears shone in Heather's eyes, and she returned the pressure.

Lina released her friend's hand. "You go about your packing," she said briskly to hide her emotion. "I have letters to write." She picked up her Bible from the small table next to her bed and, using it as a temporary desk, wrote her response to Trudy.

Dear Trudy,

I have accepted Mr. Barrett's proposal! I must say having your letter considerably eased my mind about giving myself in matrimony to a man I did not know. Because of your words and his own, Mr. Barrett does not feel like a stranger, but someone I could admire and find happiness with. I feel as if I love little Adam already, and I can't wait to hug him and shower his sweet face with kisses.

Thank you, my dear Trudy, for thinking of me. How wonderful it will be to live in the same town—to know I am among friends and not strangers.

I hope to see you when I arrive on the 18th of June.

Your friend in affection,

Lina Napolitano

☙

The next day, Lina rushed into the agency house, breathless from an early morning journey to her family's home. She wanted to send off Heather with a wedding present of a brooch but hadn't been able to find the trinket.

At home, her mama and younger sisters had helped her search. Her two sisters had chattered on about Heather and Lina's weddings, while her mama worked grim-faced. Mama didn't approve of Lina's decision. She didn't want her daughter to marry a man who wasn't first approved by her papá, who wasn't Catholic—Jonah's willingness to convert wasn't good enough—and who lived so far away.

Heather walked down the stairs, a carpetbag in one hand, her coat draped over the other arm. She wore a skirt and blouse of jade serge, which made her eyes look vibrant. Her trunk already stood near the doorway. "There you are!" she exclaimed, a look of relief crossing her face. "Lina, where have you been? I looked everywhere for you. I thought I'd have to leave without saying goodbye, which distressed me immensely."

"I'm so sorry, Heather." Lina rushed over to her friend. "I didn't mean to take so long. Last night before I fell asleep, I thought how nice taking a keepsake from me would be, so I rushed home to give you a brooch of mine." She frowned. "I couldn't find it. Searched everywhere. Turns out my oldest sister borrowed the pin, but she doesn't know what she did with it. I'll have to send it to you later."

"Oh, Lina!" Heather's green eyes filled with tears. She set down her carpetbag and gave Lina a long hug. "You mustn't. I have nothing for you."

"Silly, your friendship is enough." Lina tightened her arms.

"I'm going to miss you so much!"

Lina kissed Heather's cheek. "May St. Christopher keep you safe on your journey. Write as soon as you can." She sniffed and dashed a finger under her eyes.

"May you find wedded happiness, Lina."

"You too, my dear Heather." She gave her friend a tremulous smile. As Heather walked out the door, Lina picked up her skirts and hurried up the stairs, to the privacy of her room.

Chapter Five

In the warmth of the June sunshine, Jonah reined in at the train depot, Adam perched in the saddle in front of him. Cawing sounds made him glance up at the water tower, where a flock of crows had gathered, perched on the railing around the bottom and looked as if they were prepared to gossip about any passengers who arrived or departed on the next train.

The terse telegram he'd received from his mail-order bride had provided no details beyond her arrival date, but Trudy had assured him Lina would write him a more personal letter. Jonah had been too busy until today to travel to town and see if he'd received her letter.

He swung off his mount, tied the reins to the hitching post, and reached up for Adam. Carrying his son, he strode up the steps to the platform and crossed the space to the brown-painted station. Once inside, he walked to the counter. Seeing no one around, Jonah peered over the side to see Stationmaster Jack Waite asleep in a worn leather chair. He cleared his throat.

Jack opened his eyes, ran a hand through his bushy salt-and-pepper hair, and stood, suppressing a yawn. He was a short man; rheumatism was beginning to twist his fingers. He peered at Jonah, no sign of recognition on his face. "How can I help you, son?"

"Jonah Barrett here to see if I've received any mail." His plain words belied the jitters in his midsection.

"Ah." The man's expression came awake. "Tell me where you live?"

Jonah held Adam in one arm, and with the other, pointed in the direction of his farm. "Out a couple of miles, near the Dunn ranch but farther into the forest."

"Good to know, good to know, Mr. Barrett," the stationmaster mumbled, as if fixing Jonah's farm on his mental map. "Got your letter right here." He walked over to a crate on the end of the counter. "This is where I keep the mail for anyone I don't know." He shuffled through a few envelopes. "Here you go." He placed the letter on the counter. "Came in yesterday."

"Thank you."

Jack tapped a second box. "Now that I know you, this is where your mail will be. You expecting more?"

"Maybe I am." Jonah hovered on the edge of silence, aware he had a decision to make. He'd sent for a bride to make some changes in his life, and that meant he'd need to be more sociable with the townsfolk. *Starting now.* "I'm expecting a mail-order bride on the eighteenth."

Jack's eyes lit, and he smacked a palm on the counter. "Well then, I can tell you now. You're going to need your own mailbox. Trudy Flanigan caught me unprepared, what with her letters going back and forth to St. Louis, Missouri and Y Knot, Montana. Didn't realize there'd be so much correspondence." He patted the top of the box. "Filled this right up, she did. And I had to make a special box for *Flanigan.*" He pointed to the shelves behind him. "Won't have that problem again. I'll have a box for you before your bride steps foot in Sweetwater Springs. What's her name? I need to know the before and after, just in case."

Jonah had to smile at the stationmaster's enthusiasm about making a mailbox. The man certainly took his job seriously. "Miss Lina, ah, Angelina Napolitano."

"Pretty. Guess you and the little one could use an angel in your lives."

With a long, slow nod, Jonah had to agree. "I guess I'll be seeing you again, Mr. Waite."

"Jack, make it, Jack. And I'll call you—"

"Jonah." He patted Adam's head. "My son Adam."

"All right, then Jonah. 'Til next time."

Feeling he'd made a start at town relations, Jonah walked into the main room of the station to seek a quiet spot where he could read his letter. Taking a look around and seeing nothing Adam could get into or hurt himself on, Jonah set down the boy and allowed him to toddle around the room. Hoping with some dread that Miss Lina hadn't changed her mind, he took a seat on one of the benches, opened the letter, and began to read.

Mr. Barrett,

After receiving your letter and the one Trudy wrote me on your behalf, I have given your situation the due consideration I believe it deserves. When I read Trudy's description of your son, I did not envision a "half-breed," as you described, but a child I could take into my arms and from there into my heart. I give you my solemn word of honor that I will respect Adam's heritage. But I will also look forward to offering him (and you, as well) my Italian heritage—the warmth, the language, and the food. As my papá is fond of saying, you haven't lived until you've eaten Italian cooking!

I have promised my family that I will spend a few more days with them before leaving for Sweetwater Springs. Expect me on the 18th of June.

Yours,

Angelina (Lina) Napolitano

Short and to the point. Jonah liked Lina's determined attitude about Adam. He reread the letter and found himself wishing she'd written more about herself.

Guess I'll have to learn more about Lina Napolitano on my own. For the first time, a bit of excitement stirred in him, bringing a small smile to his lips.

Lina had just finished helping the cook prepare for dinner when Mrs. Seymour came in the door, an envelope in her hand. "This is for you, Lina."

Lina took the letter and glanced at the front. *From Heather!* She'd missed her friend but hadn't dared hope to hear from her so soon. "Thank you, Mrs. Seymour." Not wanting to wait until she climbed all the way to the attic dormitory, Lina moved into the parlor, took the pointed letter opener from a shelf of the secretary, and slit open the top of the envelope. Once the letter was free, Lina crossed the room to perch on the edge of the brown velvet settee and began to read.

> *Dear Lina,*
>
> *Please do not be alarmed when I tell you Hayden Klinkner is nowhere to be found. I hope he is just late in arriving. Feeling a bit self-conscious standing alone on the street with my trunk, I ducked into the mercantile to gather my wits. When I noticed a mail counter I thought of you—St. Louis, my family and friends. Everything I left behind. I am trying not to feel lost. But I shall not judge too harshly, for some wayward event may have postponed him. Surely, I am being rash, for he is only half an hour overdue.*
>
> *Please keep this to yourself. I do not want to worry Mrs. Seymour or the girls. I apologize for this brief note. Hopefully, Hayden will arrive before this letter is even posted. I will write more once I get settled—somewhere...*
>
> *Love,*
> *Heather*

Lina gasped, felt a rush of concern squeeze her ribcage, and reread the letter, paying particular attention to the date. When she finished, although wanting to do something, she sat on the settee, feeling helpless. *Did Hayden Klinkner ever show up? Is Heather still alone?*

Heather had forbidden her to talk to the other brides or Mrs. Seymour, and Lina didn't know where else to turn. All of a sudden, Montana seemed so far away.

All I can do is pray.

Lina jumped to her feet and rushed up the back stairway to

her room. She tried not to glance at the empty bed next to hers for it only made her miss Heather and grabbed for her black shawl, hanging on a peg next to her red one, then tied on her best bonnet. She took her crocheted reticule, hearing the clink of coins inside. From habit, she tucked in a clean handkerchief and then added Heather's folded letter.

Grateful for the good weather, Lina hurried out the door of the agency, down the walkway, and through the gate to the street. She was so absorbed in her thoughts—in her need to get to church to light a candle for Heather, that she barely paid attention to her surroundings beyond dodging other pedestrians. Since living at the agency, she'd only attended mass at St. Anthony's a few times, preferring to take a street car to her neighborhood and attend St. Francis of Assisi with family members. As she hurried up the walkway of the brick church, she almost bumped into a man coming in the other direction.

"Whoa, Miss Lina." A hand steadied her.

Hearing her name, she looked up to see Morgan Stanford, Heather's brother, staring down at her. She blinked to focus her vision. The tall man had dark hair and green eyes like his sister, and also like Heather's, they gleamed with laughter.

The sight of him sent Lina's thoughts scurrying. Heather hadn't said she couldn't confide in her brother. *Dare I?* "What are you doing here, Mr. Stanford?"

"Father Michael's hack threw a shoe. I brought the gelding to the shop, shod the horse, and just returned it to the rectory stable. Our family takes care of the mounts of all the clergy in the area." As Morgan watched her, the amusement faded from his eyes. "Is everything all right, Miss Lina?"

"It's Heather," she blurted out. She fumbled with the strings of her reticule and handed over her friend's letter.

Morgan read the words on the page, a frown pulling at his handsome face. When he finished, he handed back the letter. "I'll take care of this, Miss Lina. I've been thinking about heading out West anyway." He pulled out his pocket watch. "I think I can pack and catch the afternoon train."

Lina clapped her hands together. "Oh, Mr. Stanford. You relieve my mind."

"Hopefully my sister hasn't gotten herself in trouble," he said, his tone grim.

Lina placed a hand on his arm. "I thought the same thing, Mr. Stanford. That's why I'm going to light a candle for her. But now that I've had a chance to calm down, I've remembered Evie Holcomb lives in Y Knot. If Hayden Klinkner doesn't show up, Heather can go stay with her."

"That's true." His expression cleared. "But I still need to check on her. Ease my mind. What about you, Miss Lina? Has Mrs. Seymour made you a match yet?"

"In two days, I'm going to Montana. Not to Y Knot, though. But at least Heather and I will be in the same territory and perhaps can visit."

He touched a finger to the brim of his hat. "Then I'll wish you good fortune."

"And to you, Mr. Stanford." Lina nodded and started up the walkway to the church. She still had a candle to light. Two candles, actually. She could use one for herself as well.

Chapter Six

Jonah stood in front of the wardrobe in his bedroom, the fanciest object in his house, made two years ago by his neighbor Gideon Walker in exchange for a pig. To make the piece significant for Koko, Gid had carved symbols—a circle and triangle that represented the sun and moon—on the outside, the same ones that were painted on her family's tipi. When Gideon had brought the piece over, quiet Koko had showed some rare emotion, tracing the symbols with her fingertips, her dark eyes moist.

A bittersweet memory.

He glanced at Adam, asleep on the bed, arms and legs sprawled, one hand in a fist. In another few hours, the boy would have a new mother, and Jonah would again have a wife. He'd made all the basic arrangements by letter with Father Fredrick, and Seth and Trudy were to meet him at the church.

His heart heavy, Jonah reached inside the wardrobe for his best shirt and, in the process, his hand brushed against the deerskin leggings and long shirt Koko had made for him to wear at their wedding. The outfit was fringed and beaded, with rows of quills down the front of the shirt. She'd been very proud of her artistry, and he'd donned the gift with pleasure and wore it for the ceremony and later for special occasions with her family.

Jonah moved on to the next garment and stopped. Koko's clothes still hung in the wardrobe, both the every day unornamented buckskin she preferred to wear at home and the calico dress he'd ordered for her from a catalogue, which she'd worn on the two times she'd visited the town.

He should have packed away Koko's things and his wedding attire before now, but Jonah hadn't been able to bear the thought. He looked around the room for inspiration, then thought of the leather box under the bed. She'd brought it with her when she came to live with him, and they'd used it for extra storage. He got to his knees, pulled out the box, and placed it on the bed. Lifting the top, he saw a flute that had been Koko's uncle's before he died. She'd wanted Adam to learn how to play the instrument when he grew old enough.

Leaving the flute in place, Jonah took the garments from the wardrobe, folded them, and set them in the box. As he finished with the last piece, a splattering sound on the roof made him glance out the window. Seeing the raindrops and the looming black clouds, he groaned. With his cursed luck, he should have anticipated bad weather.

Now what am I going to do?

Jonah spared a thought for Seth and Trudy and wondered if they'd make it to town in this downpour. He'd arranged with the Flanigans to bring Lina home in their wagon after the wedding ceremony. Trudy was sure Lina couldn't ride horseback, and Jonah didn't have a wagon. He and Koko had ridden their horses everywhere they went.

He knew Seth had the ribs and canvas to make a covered wagon, which would keep the women fairly dry inside. But his friend on the driver's seat would only have a hat and slicker to shield him from the rain. Showing up to the wedding during a storm was beyond the call of friendship, and he felt bad about putting the couple out.

But how else can I get Lina home? Jonah groaned. *This is not a good way to start a marriage.*

He glanced at his sleeping son, wishing he didn't have to

bring him out in the wet weather. Adam would probably be better off wearing the buckskin clothing his mother had made him. Then if Jonah bundled the child in the canvas and held the boy in front of him on the horse... He would have preferred not to introduce Adam to his new mother when he was wearing Indian garments, but the boy's health came first. But what if the sight of the child dressed that way put Lina off?

With a sinking feeling Jonah realized that everything about his wedding day would be a disaster—not unlike the whole course of his life. He thought of Koko, dead in childbirth, and wondered if God was warning him off taking another wife. By marrying him, Lina was aligning herself with a man with the Biblical misfortune of his namesake. Could he do that to an innocent woman?

He glanced over at his sleeping son, and his throat tightened. *I have no choice.*

☙

Lina stared out the train window—not that she could see much through the rain-smudged glass—holding her rosary in one hand. The other anchored a shallow wooden crate to her lap, filled with soil and growing herbs.

The gray outside misted her view of the passing landscape and pervaded her spirits. In all her daydreams about meeting her husband and stepson and the subsequent wedding ceremony, she'd never imagined rain—not just a drizzle, but pouring rain. And in spite of the stern talking-to she gave herself, Lina couldn't help feeling the weather was an ill-omen for her marriage. In an attempt to assuage her fears, she fingered the rosary beads, saying a Hail Mary on each.

The conductor, wearing a black slicker over his uniform, walked down the aisle. "Next stop, Sweetwater Springs." He paused at Lina's row. "Why don't you give me the box, Miss? That way you can handle..." He waved to the enamel pot on the seat next to her filled with braided ropes of garlic, a block of

Parmesan cheese, cloth bags, small bottles of dried Italian herbs, and a few other items.

Grateful to hand over the burden that had rested on her lap since she'd left St. Louis, Lina gave him the box. The only reason she'd brought along the little garden was because her nonna had, with her own gnarled hands, transplanted the herbs from her yard into the crate and insisted Lina bring them on the trip. Nonna might be seventy-two years old, but, as the family matriarch, all her children, grandchildren, and great-grandchildren obeyed her every command.

Lina hurriedly untied the gray grosgrain ribbons on her small straw hat, pulling it off and smoothing her hair. Some of her curls had escaped the hairpins holding the mass back in a low bun, and she tucked them in, only to have the tendrils spring forth again. Sighing, she gave up.

Rummaging in her valise, Lina pulled out a little paper packet and unfolded the edges to reveal a red sateen ribbon. She waved her hat back and forth to dislodge any stray ashes from the smoke belching out of the smokestack and drifting in through any open window. Once the brim was cleaner, she exchanged the gray ribbon for the red. No matter what clothing she wore, Lina liked to have a touch of red on her—ribbons or an artificial peony—knowing the color brightened her complexion and complimented her dark coloring. She'd worn the gray ones for traveling because she didn't want to ruin her red ones.

Not for the first time, Lina wondered what Jonah Barrett would think of her arriving with a box of plants and a heavy pot. But her mama had insisted she take the pot, and like Nonna, Maria Napolitano couldn't be gainsaid. If Lina was going to haul around the pot anyway, she might as well fill the interior with those various items that might leave an unsavory odor among her dresses and delicates in the trunk.

The train slowed to a stop. The downpour was so heavy, mingled with steam from the train, that she could see nothing of her new community—a community that might snub her for having a half-breed son. Feeling reluctance and anticipation, she stood, brushed off her coat, and picked up the valise.

A few feet away, the conductor waited patiently.

When Lina was ready, she gave him a nod and handed him the herb box. Then she grasped her valise in one hand and her pot in the other.

Holding the herb box, the conductor slid in between two empty seats and gestured to her to go ahead of him.

When she reached the exit, Lina took a deep breath and stepped onto the wooden platform and into rainy Sweetwater Springs.

Chapter Seven

Outside the train station, Jonah reined in near the back of the Flanigans' covered wagon. He dismounted, using a square of canvas draped over Adam's head to keep the rain from hitting the boy's face. The movement woke his son, who'd fallen asleep again on the ride to town.

The child began to cry.

As he tried to keep the protection over the boy, Jonah found his boots sinking into several inches of mud. He bit off a curse and jiggled Adam, hoping to get him to stop crying. But the effort just made the boy raise his voice.

Seth snapped open a black umbrella and held it over the back of the wagon.

Trudy undid the rope tying the canvas closed, pushed the opening wider, and climbed out, helped by her husband. She was dressed in a hooded woolen cloak and carried some red flowers.

At first, Jonah thought they were roses. But then she moved, and he saw they were peonies.

"Oh, Adam," Trudy cooed at the boy. "Don't cry, sweetie."

To Jonah's surprise, the boy's sobs faded to sniffles.

Trudy thrust the peonies into Jonah's free hand. "For you to give to Lina. They're her favorite." She slanted a teasing smile up at her husband. "*Someone* didn't greet me with flowers when I arrived, and I was a little disappointed."

"I made up for the oversight," Seth pointed out. "If I hadn't gone to Mrs. Cameron to beg for roses for the ceremony, the Camerons and Carters wouldn't have been at our wedding. So you ended up with flowers *and* new friends. I consider that a bonus."

Trudy smiled. "I wouldn't have had it any other way."

In spite of the rain dripping around her and the chill in the air, the expression of love on Trudy's face when she gazed up at her husband made an ache somewhere in the vicinity of Jonah's heart. He and Koko had established a relationship of caring and respect, one he'd thought was complete. He'd never even considered the kind of love Seth and Trudy displayed...never knew to even hope for it. And he didn't allow himself to do so now. "Let's head on up," he said, his voice gruff.

At the stairs to the platform, Jonah tried to knock the mud off his boots on the edge of the first step, but the movement made the canvas slip from Adam's head. In hastily pulling the covering back over his son, he dropped one of the flowers. He couldn't crouch to pick it up without getting Adam wet. Maybe Trudy wouldn't notice.

Seth and Trudy climbed to the platform behind him, then moved to his side. Trudy had taken charge of the umbrella, and Seth kept one arm around her waist.

Jonah juggled Adam and the flowers. He hoped Lina wouldn't expect any romantic gesture like him taking her hand, or even worse, kissing her. Even if he were inclined to do so, his hands were full.

With a head of steam from the chimney and a whoosh of brakes, the train pulled into the station. The sight and noise of the monster train frightened Adam, and he set up a wail. Jonah half-turned to block the boy's view of the train. A gust of wind from behind belled the bottom of Jonah's slicker and lifted the back of his hat a few inches—enough to expose his unprotected neck. The forward tilt of his hat blocked his vision, so he didn't see Lina descending from the train.

"Lina!" Trudy called out to her friend. She broke away from the shelter of Seth's arm and hurried forward.

Hastily, Jonah used his forearm to push back his hat, dropping a few more peonies in the process and breaking the stem of another until it drooped forlornly to one side.

Adam's crying sounded heartbreaking.

He jiggled the boy, trying to soothe him.

The movement only served to anger his normally placid son. Adam took a swat at his father and in the process sheared one of the four remaining blossoms from the stem.

Embarrassed, Jonah surveyed the sorry-looking bouquet, wondering if he should still give the flowers to Lina or toss them under the platform. If Trudy weren't here, he'd do the latter. But he didn't want to offend the wife of his friend.

Trudy stepped to the train, sharing the protection of her umbrella with Lina.

A little irked that he hadn't been the one to first greet the woman—not that he'd want her to get wet—Jonah strode forward. The rain and the umbrella blocking his view made seeing his mail-order bride difficult, but he noticed she carried an enamel pot, which seemed to be filled with packages.

"Let me take that from you." Seth reached for Lina's valise."

The umbrella tilted back, and Jonah caught a glimpse of big, dark eyes before the edge dipped again, and he lost sight of her. A little bewildered by Lina's choice of a pot for luggage, he pushed the scraggly bouquet in the direction of her gloved hand. "Welcome," the word came out in a monotone.

There was no response, although she took hold of the stems.

Fearing Lina hadn't even heard him, Jonah repeated the single word, raising his voice over the rain tap-tapping around them. *Do I sound ridiculous, greeting her twice?*

In his preoccupation with the flowers, Jonah loosened his hold on the canvas around Adam's head. The covering slipped off and fluttered to the ground, landing in a puddle where it flattened as the material soaked up water.

The downpour slicked Adam's hair to his head, which only made him increase the volume of his screams.

Jonah took off his hat and held it over his son's head. The rain plastered his hair to his neck.

The conductor stepped from the train carrying a large flat crate.

Were those plants inside that box?

Looking around, the man focused on Seth as the only one with a free hand and thrust the crate at him. "Best of luck, Miss," he called before getting back on the train, escaping the downpour.

❦

Relieved to feel the warmth and welcome of friendship, Lina emerged from Trudy's enthusiastic embrace, desperately wanting to see Jonah and Adam. But what the umbrella didn't block from her view, the rain did. All she could see was a man in a cowboy hat holding a squirming bundle, covered in canvas, who issued unhappy shrieks.

Her fingers itched to reach for the child to see if she could comfort him.

A leather-gloved hand thrust a pathetic bouquet of stems at her, from which dangled a few mangled peony blossoms. Even as she looked at them, one flower detached and drifted to the ground, leaving behind only two. A sweet gesture to be sure, but she wondered what had happened to the rest.

"This is my husband, Seth," Trudy said in a voice loud enough to be heard over the noise of the crying baby and pounding rain. "Husband, this is my dear friend Angelina Napolitano." She patted the arm of the man next to her. "And this is Jonah Barrett and little Adam."

"How do you do, Miss Napolitano?" said Seth.

Lina peered around the edge of the umbrella and caught a glimpse of a blond beard. The spray of rain hitting her face made her duck back under the umbrella.

Seth bent lower to make eye contact. "Do you have more luggage?"

"A trunk."

He glanced at the crate in his arms, then at Jonah holding the baby. "I'll come back for the trunk. Let's get you all to the Nortons."

Trudy pulled on Lina's arm, and the two of them huddled together under the umbrella, trotting to the end of the platform and down the stairs. The pot thumped against her leg.

Lina's feet sank into several inches of mud. With the hand holding the bouquet, she grabbed up her skirt before the hem became dirty. *Good thing I wore sturdy boots instead of my nice ones.*

They trudged down the street through the mud, the two women in front, the men following. The wails of the baby accompanied them all the way.

Poor bambino! Lina longed to take Adam in her arms and comfort him. Perhaps when they reached shelter, Mr. Barrett would allow her to hold his son.

The more they walked, the wetter they became. Trudy tried, not always successfully, to steer them around puddles and keep the umbrella over both their heads. From time to time, she'd name the building they passed… "Mercantile. Hardy's Saloon, don't go near there."

Through the pouring rain, Lina could only glimpse hazy outlines of dark structures. The storm made everything, even the white schoolhouse they passed, seem gray and desolate.

As Lina tried to keep the heavy pot from banging into her leg, her arm grew tired and started to ache, and her fingers cramped. Attempting to hold the hem of her skirt out of the mud with her other hand made leaning in toward Trudy under the umbrella awkward. She could feel the rain penetrating her hat and knew the brim was probably drooping. She hoped it wasn't ruined.

Her dread grew with each step. *What have I done?* Lina fervently wished she were back home in St. Louis, tucked in an armchair in front of the fire, with the smell of her mama's red sauce simmering on the kitchen stove and the warmth of her family surrounding her.

Trudy took an abrupt left turn at a white clapboard building. The umbrella dipped to the side and a gust of wind blew rain in their faces. "I'm so sorry you're having to practically *swim* to the parsonage."

Lina blinked to clear her eyes and realized they were rounding a church.

"We're almost there, thank goodness," Trudy said in her ear. *Thank goodness, indeed.*

In a few more steps, they came to a small house. She caught a glimpse of a cemetery on the other side. They hurried up the stairs to the porch. Trudy lowered the umbrella and set it down in the corner to dry off. The men crowded behind them under the shelter of the roof.

As Seth set the garden box on the other corner of the porch, the door flew open and an older woman in a plain gray dress and white apron appeared, gesturing for them to enter. "Come in out of this nasty weather." She stood aside and waited for everyone to traipse through the doorway.

"This is Mrs. Norton," Trudy said to Lina as they passed by the woman. "Miss Angelina Napolitano. We call her Lina."

"Miss Napolitano," said Mrs. Norton, all but bobbing a curtsy.

Adam continued his pathetic crying.

"Oh, the poor dear boy. Let's get him warm and dry. Mrs. Flanigan, dear, please lead the way to the kitchen."

Feeling as if her arm was going to fall off, Lina followed Trudy down a hallway. She didn't dare look to see how much mud they were tracking onto Mrs. Norton's floor.

Trudy turned left into a warm kitchen, filled with the aroma of roasting chicken and baking bread.

Lina inhaled the homey scents, feeling some of her tenseness leave her. *Almost as welcoming as the smell of red sauce and pasta noodles.*

With a sigh of relief, she set the pot on the table and made to tuck her bouquet inside, then realized she only had one flower left, clinging to a stem, and one other crushed between the leaves. Lina gently touched the petal of the intact blossom. She'd wear it for the wedding ceremony and later, she'd press the bloom between the pages of her bible. *Provided it survives the day.* Setting down the peony, she pulled off her gloves and balled them into her pocket, before sliding the coat off her shoulders.

She caught a glimpse of the bearded man who held his crying son.

Mrs. Norton held out a hand distracting her. "Here, Miss Napolitano, let me take that for you." The minister's wife was a slight woman with kind blue eyes. When she smiled, wrinkles formed around her eyes and mouth. Her brown hair, liberally streaked with gray, was pulled back in a tight bun. She hung the coat on one of a row of pegs by the door. "The rest of you can put your things here as well."

Trudy hung up her coat.

Seth set Lina's valise near the doorway.

Mrs. Norton waved to a stack of towels in a pile on the table. "Dry off. Then come sit near the stove and warm up. Reverend Norton is in his office finishing his next sermon. He'll be out soon."

Jonah dropped the piece of canvas he'd used to protect Adam onto the floor underneath their coats and hung his hat on a peg. His blond hair was darkened with rainwater. One-armed, he awkwardly unwrapped the blanket from around his son, which only increased Adam's wails.

For the first time, Lina had a good look at the boy, and she centered all her attention on him.

Adam's dark hair was wet and his face scrunched and red. He was dressed in odd clothes that looked like soft leather. His green eyes were drenched, the long lashes clumped together. Snot ran from his nose. He was the very picture of almost-two-year-old misery.

Yearning ran through her, so powerful it tore at her heart. She longed to take him in her arms and calm him.

Mrs. Norton's hands fluttered. "Is Adam hungry, Mr. Barrett? I have some mashed potatoes."

"He ate before we left home."

"How about his diaper?" Lina asked.

"He's pretty good about using the pot." Mr. Barrett stood the boy on a chair, pulled his leggings away from his bottom and peered inside. Apparently not seeing a messy diaper, he stuck a finger down Adam's pants. "He's dry."

The procedure only made Adam's wails become louder.

Lina couldn't stand it for another minute. She held out her hands. "Let me try. Please, Mr. Barrett?" She saw the indecision in his eyes but kept her arms extended.

With a small nod, he handed his son to her.

Adam stiffened. He leaned away from her and held out one hand to his father, fingers spread in entreaty.

Mr. Barrett moved to take him back.

Lina shook her head, then turned and walked to the other side of the kitchen. Mrs. Norton gave her a scrap of cloth, and she cleaned the boy's nose. Then she faced the window, her full attention on the babe in her arms. Rocking him back and forth, she crooned, "Shush, shush, *carissimo*, shush." She uttered a string of soft Italian words she'd heard all her life to soothe upset babies.

Adam's body softened against her, but his wails did not cease.

Lina continued a flow of gentle words, at the same time rubbing circles on his back with the palm of her hand.

Adam gave a hiccuping sob. His cries quieted to sniffles that shook his whole body.

"There, there." Lina switched to English. "You're all right." She patted his back.

With a shuddering sob, Adam relaxed and laid his head on her shoulder.

"Ah." Lina brushed a hand over the back of his head. "That's better." She dropped a kiss on his forehead, inhaling his little boy smell. His weight settled against her, familiar and so very right.

From the time she was a young girl, Lina had held and

rocked babies. There were always plenty of little ones around in her family, and she loved them all. But nothing had prepared her for the fierce stab of maternal love that pierced her heart, so deeply she almost ached with the pain and joy of the feeling. Hot tears sprang to her eyes. *This child is mine!*

Holding her son to her breast, Lina turned and looked at the four adults watching her. "I'm his *mother*," she said in wonder. One statement alone wasn't enough to express the wealth of emotion...of her swift and irrevocable bond to the child. "*I'm Adam's mother!*"

Chapter Eight

Jonah stared at the woman who'd just staked her claim to his son. An Italian Madonna, with lambent eyes bright with tears, stood before him, possessive energy crackling in the air.

In that moment, feeling lighter than he had in months, Jonah realized he could lay down the burden of uncertainty and dread he'd carried ever since Koko's death. He let out a breath of relief that shook him to the core of his being. *I've made the right choice.* No matter what else came of his marriage, his son had a mother. And not only a woman to fill the maternal role, but…he almost smiled at the image, a mother bear who would protect her cub with teeth and claws. With her words, "I'm Adam's mother," she'd just challenged them all.

A smile pulled at the corners of his mouth. "I guess you are, at that," he agreed.

Lina gave him a tentative smile, which widened to show her dimples.

For a moment, he studied this stranger he was about to wed. Her curly hair was caught back in a thick, braided bun, and bouncy wet tendrils danced around her face. She was plump where Koko had been lithe, her face rounded instead of his wife's angular features. Koko had been almost as tall as him, whereas the top of Lina's head barely reached his shoulders.

He would have wed a hag, if she was a good mother to his boy—not that Trudy Flanigan would have matched him up with a hag. But to have a woman whose pleasant features and air of cozy competence appealed to him was an unlooked-for blessing. For the first time, Jonah found himself looking forward to his marriage—to the comforts of domesticity. He gave Lina a tentative smile, feeling as if the movement stretched facial muscles that were stiff from long disuse.

Just as quickly as he became aware of the optimistic nature of his thoughts, Jonah reined them in. He couldn't allow himself to believe his bad luck had changed. He'd done that with Koko—relaxed into the security of a family. Her death had only proven to him how he needed to always be on guard against life.

Trudy said something to Lina, he hadn't heard what.

Lina tipped back her head and laughed.

The sound of her laugh was earthy and downright infectious. He couldn't help but smile again.

Holding back may be harder than I thought.

🌀

After a burst of shared laughter, Trudy's eyes welled with tears.

"What?" Lina demanded.

Trudy sniffed. "Seeing Adam take to you…" She placed a hand over her heart. "I'm so glad…so relieved…"

Seth put an arm around his wife's shoulders and gave her a squeeze. His compelling gray eyes softened when he looked at his wife.

Trudy glanced up at him, love and gratitude on her face.

Lina caught her breath. Now it was her turn to be moved to tears. She was so grateful for the love her friend had found from her mail-order marriage.

She looked at Mr. Barrett…*Jonah*…really seeing him for the first time, not as a helpless father, but as her *mate*. Her husband-to-be was taller than most of the men in her family, but not so as to tower over her. He had a lean build, perhaps too thin. But her pasta soon would fill him out. His vivid green eyes had lost the look of melancholy they'd held earlier, and she wondered about the shape of his mouth and chin hidden by the beard. He must have trimmed his whiskers because the beard wasn't bushy, as Trudy had written. He wore his thick gold hair long to his shoulders.

Trudy dashed away a tear. "Silly, sentimental me. And here we are all standing around still wet." She picked up a towel from the table and dabbed at her face. Then she draped it over her shoulder, lifted two more and distributed them to the men. The last one she handed to Lina.

While everyone else was rubbing their heads and faces dry, Lina dabbed at Adam's face.

He wrinkled his face and shook his head.

When Lina persisted, to her relief, he didn't start crying. "Good boy." She planted a kiss on his dry cheek before running the towel gently over his head, then briskly rubbing his hair dry.

Mrs. Norton took down some soup bowls from a cupboard, placing them on the table. "While we're waiting for Reverend Norton and Father Fredrick, you all can eat something. Miss Napolitano, you must be famished."

This morning, Lina had finished off the rest of the bread she'd brought from home. But with her stomach cramped from nervousness, she wasn't sure she could eat a bite, no matter how appetizing the food smelled. And now that Adam had settled down, she didn't want to disturb him. Although, her arms were tired, she didn't mind sitting at the table while she held the child.

Mrs. Norton cast her an understanding glance. "You just have a seat here." She pulled out a chair and waved with a hand. "And perhaps just a little chicken broth for you, Miss Napolitano. The rolls I've made are soft. Perfect for dipping. You won't even have to chew. One of our parishioners dropped off a bag of white flour yesterday. Such a nice treat to bake with." As she spoke, the woman deftly set the table.

"Would you like some help, Mrs. Norton?" Trudy offered.

"No, no." The minister's wife waved to the stove. "The water in the kettle on the back of the stove is warm, but not too hot. The wash basin is over there." She pointed to a corner. "There's soap and you have towels. You can wash your hands. Ladies, there's another one in the bedroom. Mrs. Flanigan, you know the way."

Trudy took charge of pouring the water into the plain white basin for the men. Then she carried the kettle out of the kitchen. With an eyebrow cocked, Lina glanced at Mr. Barrett for permission to take Adam with her.

He nodded.

Lina followed Trudy into the bedroom.

Trudy poured water into a basin patterned with roses. She tested the temperature with the tip of her finger. "Let me take the kettle to the kitchen. I'll be right back."

Taking advantage of the moment of solitude, Lina dropped a kiss on Adam's silky head. "I'm your new *mama*," she murmured, using the Italian pronunciation. "Can you say, *mama*?"

Adam didn't answer but just looked around the room.

Lina wondered how long before she'd hear him say the word to her. *Hopefully that day will come soon!* On that thought, she had to laugh at herself. Despite all the fanciful daydreams of instant love from her stepson, she knew winning over a child often took a lot of time and patience. She'd made more progress with Adam today than she'd dared hope.

When Trudy returned, she impulsively hugged Lina, careful not to disturb the child. "I'm *so* happy you're here! I've been counting the days and wringing my hands, hoping everything will turn out well." Her voice lightened. "Do you know how hard it is to work with your hands tied up that way?"

Lina laughed.

At the sound, Adam stared at her with wide eyes.

Smiling again, Lina kissed his forehead. "It's time for you to hear more laughter, my son."

Trudy dipped in a washcloth and wrung it out. "Seeing you with Adam has made me confident everything will work out for your marriage."

"A husband's different than a baby." A twinge of uneasiness went through her.

Trudy's eyes twinkled. "Thank goodness for that!" She handed the washcloth to Lina. "Adam probably won't stand for me to do it, but since you have the magic touch…"

Lina gently dabbed the cloth on Adam's cheek.

He scrunched his face and tried to turn away.

Trudy stood at the basin and washed her hands, drying them on the towel hanging from a rail.

Deftly, Lina finished Adam's face, relieved he didn't start crying. "Let's try this." She gave him to Trudy.

Trudy rocked him with gentle movements. "I haven't held a little one in ages."

Lina dipped her hands in the water, grabbed the soap, and lathered. *Oh, to be rid of the cinders and smoke!*

Adam made a noise of distress.

Lina glanced over her shoulder. "I'm hurrying, *carissimo*."

Trudy rocked him. "It's all right, Adam. Your mama's almost finished."

Squirming, he started to cry.

Wanting to comfort the boy and concerned that his father out in the kitchen might hear his distress and think she was doing something wrong, Lina splashed some water on her face. She took the towel and quickly dried her face and hands.

"Let me fold that," Trudy offered. "You take him."

Lina dropped the cloth on the washstand and held out her hands to the little boy.

Adam leaned toward her, arms out.

The gesture made a rush of love go through her. She took him into her arms and gave him a kiss. "Let's go find your *papà*."

Chapter Nine

Everyone took a seat around the table and bowed their heads while Mrs. Norton said grace, asking God's blessing for the food and for the marriage of Miss Napolitano to Mr. Barrett.

The simple prayer made a feeling of peace well up in Lina. She crossed herself. When she lifted her head, she saw Jonah studying her. She blushed and looked away.

Mrs. Norton took a spoonful of soup, and everyone else followed suit.

Lina had plenty of practice holding and feeding a little one while at the same time trying to eat. She set Adam on her left side, broke off a piece of roll and let him gnaw on it while she took a few spoonfuls of soup. The broth was warm and rich, the thick noodles different than the pasta she was familiar with.

Between sips of soup and bites of buttered rolls, Mrs. Norton and the Flanigans took turns filling in Lina about the inhabitants of Sweetwater Springs.

Mr. Barrett remained silent, although he sometimes nodded at something one of the others said. But mostly, he watched Lina and Adam with solemn green eyes.

His scrutiny made her uncomfortable. She couldn't tell if he approved of her actions with Adam or not. Lina supposed he must feel somewhat comfortable, or he would have taken back the boy. But then again, he might not want to embarrass her in front of the others by doing so.

Slow footsteps sounded in the hall, and Reverend Norton entered the kitchen. He had gray-threaded dark hair and penetrating blue eyes. A trimmed beard failed to soften his austere features. He was dressed in a black frock coat over gray trousers. His grave expression didn't change when he saw her.

Lina shivered, wondering if the minister disapproved of Catholics. In some parts of St. Louis, the tension between the Catholics and the Protestants ran high, often resulting in fisticuffs. Any Protestant minister would condemn Jonah's intent to convert, and she tensed, bracing for Reverend Norton's reaction.

Mrs. Norton waved her spoon at Lina. "This is Miss Angelina Napolitano, our bride."

He nodded a greeting, a worried look in his eyes. "Miss Napolitano, I'm afraid this storm is not the welcoming weather you would have wished for on your wedding day."

Lina glanced around at her companions, smiling at each one. "Oh, I don't know. The weather is miserable, but the welcome from the Flanigans, from Mrs. Norton, has been everything I could possibly desire." She sent Jonah a small smile. "Mr. Barrett greeted me with a beautiful bouquet of flowers." She jiggled the boy. "Adam, here, has allowed me to hold him. So I'm counting my blessings."

His eyes softened. "That attitude does you well." He looked at Jonah. "Clearly, the weather has delayed Father Fredrick's arrival. On his visits to Sweetwater Springs, he aims to be here early so he can partake of Mrs. Norton's cooking."

Mrs. Norton waved her spoon in a back-and-forth, *no, no* motion. "Now, Reverend Norton. You know as well as I do that Father Fredrick wants to make sure he's available for anyone needing to speak with him before mass."

"I do know, my dear. I was trying to inject a little levity into a situation that might cause Miss Napolitano some distress." He looked at Lina and frowned. "I've sent someone to check the level of the river. He'll see if Father Fredrick's mule will be able to cross at the ford. We should have word soon."

What does he mean, Father Fredrick might be delayed? Will this cancel the ceremony?

Reverend Norton gestured to the table. "Please, continue. I'll wash up and join you." He turned and left the room.

Mrs. Norton rose and went to the stove to ladle out a bowl of soup for her husband.

"Why was Father Fredrick across the river?" Lina asked. "I hope he didn't have to go administer last rites to some poor soul."

Silence met her question. Trudy and Lina exchanged puzzled looks.

Finally, Mrs. Norton spoke. "Father Fredrick ministers to four different towns. In good weather, he spends a few days at each place before moving on. He has to travel for several days to reach some of the more remote areas. Towns so tiny, they don't even have a minister. From time to time, Reverend Norton drives out to them. But he has his hands full just administering to Sweetwater Springs and the outlying areas."

Lina drew in a sharp breath of dismay. In St. Louis, you could find a Catholic church every square mile or so. "You mean Father Fredrick doesn't reside here?"

"No, Miss Napolitano. I'm sorry."

Lina couldn't absorb the distressing news. "There's no Catholic church? No daily mass? I can't light candles when I need to say a special prayer?"

Mrs. Norton gazed at her, compassion in her eyes. "I'm afraid not, my dear. Father Frederick tries to hold mass once a month, but with weather and other obstacles..." She spread her hands in a helpless gesture.

Pressure banded around Lina's chest. Panicked, she sent Trudy a glance of appeal.

Her friend stared at her with wide eyes, her hand raised almost to her mouth. "I'm so sorry, Lina. I didn't know... I mean, I knew there was only one church...but..." She glanced at

Seth. "When we stayed late in town last month after the service, we saw people gathering for mass. I had no idea that didn't happen every week."

Her husband shook his head. "And I didn't think to tell you." Seth gave a helpless shrug. "We've lived here all our lives—taken things for granted." He exchanged concerned glances with Jonah.

Remorse showed in her bridegroom's eyes. "We don't really know another way of doing things...what it's like to live in a city with more than one church, different ways..."

Lina's thoughts whirled. Her heart raced, and she wanted to rush out of the room, run away to think. She glanced out the window, blurry with water rivulets. But she didn't know where she'd go, even if the rain wasn't pouring down outside. And...most importantly, the baby's weight in her lap anchored her to the chair. *I'm a mother now. I can't go running off when I get upset. Somehow, for Adam's sake, I must come to terms with this.*

Trudy reached across the table to touch her hand. "I feel terrible, Lina...as though I've misled you."

She tried to swallow, to make allowances. "It's not your fault. You didn't know."

Her friend scrunched up her face. "Would it be so very bad for you to attend church with us on the other three Sundays? We could sit together," Trudy said in a hopeful tone.

"If we were home in St. Louis, I know my priest, Father Daren, would say no." She tried to take a deep breath through her tight chest. "Perhaps I can discuss the situation with Father Fredrick and receive his dispensation."

Just as Reverend Norton came back into the kitchen, sharp knocks sounded at the front door. He halted, furrowing his brow. "That's not Father Fredrick's knock."

Mrs. Norton started to rise, but her husband motioned her to stay. He left the room to answer the door.

Lina waited anxiously for the minister to return. She heard the distant murmur of voices, then the sound of footsteps returning to the kitchen.

Reverend Norton entered and looked at Lina, apology written on his face. "I'm sorry, Miss Napolitano. The news is… Father Fredrick cannot ford the river. The water's too high; the current's too swift."

"Oh, no," Trudy gasped.

Reverend Norton took a seat at the head of the table. "And perhaps the water will not go down enough for Father Fredrick to even make Sunday mass. The service will be delayed. Father Fredrick will say mass regardless of what day of the week it is, but I can't tell you when that will be."

No mass! No priest! Lina sat as still as a statue, feeling as if her body had turned to stone.

"Reverend Norton, what happens when there's no mass?" Trudy asked, her expression worried.

"In good weather, those in town still gather at the church for a prayer service and afterwards, they picnic together under the big tree. I'm sure other families who live a distance away mark the Sabbath with a similar ritual."

The man's words buzzed in Lina's ears, and she couldn't take in their meaning.

Reverend Norton's gaze was compassionate. "I can marry you and Mr. Barrett."

Lina instinctively shook her head.

He raised a staying hand. "Hear me out, Miss Napolitano. You'll be legally wed, which will satisfy the proprieties." He gave her a gentle smile. "And I do believe you'll be married in the eyes of God."

Attending a Protestant service was one thing. Marrying in a Protestant ceremony was an entirely different matter. Lina's heart froze. *My parents will be furious! My nonna will cry.*

"However, I know you won't feel comfortable." Reverend Norton gave her a wry smile. "Perhaps *comfortable* isn't the correct word. I'm sure this whole situation is unsettling. You won't feel *properly* married with me performing the service. Father Fredrick can conduct a Catholic ceremony when he arrives."

All Lina's hopes and dreams about her wedding had

crumbled. *This isn't how my marriage was supposed to be.* She shook her head again. "No. I can't be married in a Protestant ceremony! It would be wrong!" Resolutely, she stood and carried Adam over to Jonah. Although her heart ached to part with him, she handed the boy to his father.

Jonah stood, his expression anxious, and took Adam into his arms. "I'm sorry for all your distress, Miss Napolitano."

Her throat tight, Lina couldn't answer in acknowledgment. She could only nod. Swallowing hard, she looked at Trudy in entreaty and forced out the words. "May I stay with you?"

"Of course." Trudy rose, folding her napkin and laying it beside her bowl.

Lina reached for her hat and set it on her head, tying the ribbons under her chin. "Thank you for your hospitality, Mrs. Norton." Lina knew her tone was wooden and hoped she didn't sound ungrateful. Try as she might, she couldn't infuse life into her voice. She turned to take down her coat from the peg.

"Mmmma." Adam made a noise of distress, which almost sounded like *mama*, as if he was begging her not to leave.

Lina stilled, her fingers gripping the soggy fabric.

Adam started to cry, which quickly escalated into a heart-rending wail.

Jonah gathered his son to his chest. "Shhhh. Shhhh, son. You'll be all right. Pa's here."

Lina bit her lip, torn between wanting to go to Adam and needing to run away. *How can I possibly leave him for several days or however long before Father Fredrick arrives?*

The boy held out his arms to her, tears drenching his green eyes.

Lina wavered. She couldn't resist the boy's plea. *Adam is my son and needs me.* She took in the child's teary eyes, Jonah's worried brow. *I'm sure the Lord knows better than I how much they both need me. He knows the intentions of my heart.* She replaced her coat on the peg.

God forgive me for what I'm about to do.

Lina walked over to Jonah and held out her arms to the child. Jonah released his son to her.

Rising, she pressed the boy to her chest. "I'll do it." Lina looked at Reverend Norton. "I'll wed Mr. Barrett now."

In the Norton's bedroom, Lina opened her valise, into which she'd carefully rolled her wedding gown—a white dress, which she'd splurged on and had a dressmaker make especially for today.

She lifted the garment and tried to shake out the wrinkles.

"How pretty!" Trudy exclaimed.

Mrs. Norton reached out a hand. "Let me take that for you, Miss Napolitano. "I'll have your gown ironed in no time."

Grateful for the woman's helpfulness, Lina handed the dress over to the minister's wife.

Trudy touched the lace of the sleeve. "Dear Mrs. Norton, it was only a short time ago that you ironed my wedding gown and gave me such loving counsel. And here you are with another mail-order bride on your hands."

Mrs. Norton blushed. "My dear Mrs. Flanigan. Sweetwater Springs gained a wonderful lady on the day you married Mr. Flanigan. I predict you will become a pillar of the community." She smiled at Lina. "I've prayed for Jonah Barrett ever since he was a boy, and I'm not stopping now. But soon, I believe he'll no longer be in need of my prayers. And that dear precious child of his will have a wonderful mother."

Lina set a hand to her throat, moved by the woman's words. *What a loving spirit she is.* "Thank you, Mrs. Norton, for keeping watch over Mr. Barrett's soul for so many years."

Trudy sniffed and made a little shooing gesture, as if moving them on from sentimentality. "The men will be waiting at the church. And who knows how long Adam will want to be parted from his new mama." Trudy made a twirling motion to Lina. "Turn so I can unbutton you." She began to undo the line of buttons down the back of Lina's dress.

With her free hand, Mrs. Norton picked up the valise and set it on the bed. "Do you need anything from in here?"

"My hairbrush." Lina pulled out hairpins from her bun, and her thick braid tumbled over her shoulder. Curious to know more about Mrs. Norton, she asked, "Do you and Reverend Norton have children?"

Her blue eyes shadowed, Mrs. Norton nodded. "We have four in heaven and one on Earth. Our only living son is a missionary in Africa, and he and his wife have a baby boy."

The sadness on the woman's face made Lina reach out and squeeze her hand in sympathy. "Must be hard not to see the *bambino*." The Italian word slipped out.

"We are very proud of Joshua, of course. Such important work. But I worry, especially about the baby." She glanced in the direction of the cemetery. "Children can be so fragile. If babies die here in America, what can happen in the heat and primitive conditions of Africa?"

Poor soul. Losing four children must have been devastating. No wonder she's worried about her only grandchild.

"Does his wife come from a big family?" Lina asked. "I know my family—" she crossed herself "—is healthy. Perhaps it's the red sauce. Actually, my grandmother would say it's the minestrone—a special soup she makes that keeps us healthy. It's rare for a child to die." She thought of her brother Luigi's suicide…but he hadn't been a child. "Maybe your daughter-in-law's family comes from sturdy stock."

Mrs. Norton visibly perked up. "My daughter-in-law has four brothers and three sisters. "Perhaps you're right, dear Miss Napolitano."

Relieved to have been of some comfort, Lina, unpinned her hair, and untangled the braid. She reached for her hairbrush and tried to restore some order to the damp locks that curled around her head more tightly than usual.

"And I certainly shouldn't worry so," Mrs. Norton said. "I must trust in the Lord. And I do, I certainly do. It's just, sometimes my human frailty gets in the way." Mrs. Norton patted Lina's hand. "Not to worry, Miss Napolitano. We lost our babies before Dr. Cameron practiced here. He's an excellent doctor."

"That's good to know." Lina dreamed of the day she'd hold her own baby. With a surge of joy she thought, perhaps by this time next year, she'd have Adam hanging onto her skirts and his little brother or sister in her arms.

Only after Father Fredrick marries us, of course.

Chapter Ten

The storm showed signs of easing off. The sheeting rain had turned to a drizzle. Jonah, carrying Adam, followed Reverend Norton to the church. He paused at the stairs to kick the worst of the mud off his boots, mounted the steps, and moved through the door. He crossed the sanctuary threshold and paused, caught by an unexpected memory.

Eight-year-old Jonah walked into church beside his mother. She stopped him just inside the door. While they waited for his father to park the wagon and see to the horses, Ma smoothed her palm over his hair. Then she stepped back, laying a hand on her round belly and giving him a proud smile.

Pa joined them, gallantly extending an arm to his wife. "This will probably be our last quiet service. So we need to enjoy it." His grin stretched across his face, and he didn't look at all sorry to lose his peace.

Ma laughed, her green eyes dancing. She gave Jonah a playful look. "If he or she is anything like big brother here, I won't get to hear much of the sermon for a while. Although hopefully, this baby won't take two years to learn to be quiet during church."

"Me, Ma?" Jonah couldn't remember that far back.

"Yes, you, little noise-maker. As soon as Reverend Norton began preaching, you started crying, and I'd have to take you out."

The three of them laughed.

"I'll take him out for you, Ma. Then you don't have to miss the sermon."

She cupped his cheek with her hand. "You will be such a good big brother, Jonah. This baby will be so loved and cared for. We've certainly waited a long time for you to have a brother or sister."

"A brother!"

His parents' laugher ushered them into the church.

Adam squirmed in his arms.

With a shake of his head, Jonah brought himself back to the present. But the memory lingered. The three of them had been so happy that day—their last occasion together. Ma was close to her time, and Jonah could hardly wait. He'd wanted a brother for so long. Had even prayed for one.

After they returned home from church, his mother's pains started and the baby boy they'd all looked forward to killed her. They'd both ended up buried in a cold grave, and his father turned to drink to console himself.

But there was no consolation for me.

Jonah tried to tear his thoughts away from the old pain and guilt and hurried inside. He pulled the canvas off Adam's head and crouched to set the boy on his feet. He stayed low to make sure the child wasn't about to start crying, but the nagging thoughts of the past wouldn't leave him.

Twenty years later with Koko's death, the history of his father and of his grandfather, for that matter, had repeated itself. He'd come to have compassion for his father because of the shared misery of losing his own wife and daughter in childbirth. Jonah swallowed down old sadness.

The boy clung to his leg, looking carefully around him.

Jonah patted his pocket to make sure his mother's wedding band, worn by Koko and now about to adorn the finger of a new bride, hopefully until they both were old and gray, was still inside. He reached down to take Adam's hand. Setting his pace to the toddler's steps, they strolled up the aisle.

Reverend Norton had gone ahead and fired up the stove in the corner. The minister took a seat in the pew nearest the stove and gestured. "Come over here, Jonah. Dry off a bit."

Somewhat reluctantly, Jonah took a seat near the minister.

Adam stayed on his feet, holding to his father's knee.

"Good to have you in this church, son. It's been a while. For a long time, I've prayed to see you within these walls again."

Uncomfortable with the minister's kind words and not knowing what to say, Jonah stared down at Adam, thinking about a young boy who couldn't understand why they stopped attending church, or why he wasn't allowed to go to school anymore but had to stay home and study with his father. How he needed to forget his friends so as not to miss them. The solitary habits he'd developed out of necessity. How the saloon became his only contact with other humans. *Thank God for Seth's friendship.* The child of a saloon girl, Seth was the only youngster Jonah had associated with.

Reverend Norton waited.

Finally Jonah lifted his head. "Thank you for not giving up on me. For those years of dropping by the house, even when Pa practically ran you off with his rifle."

The older man shook his head, his mouth turned down. "I tried to persuade your father to change his mind and send you back to school. But Samuel was too bitter." He sighed. "I'm amazed you haven't absorbed his bitterness."

Haven't I? "I think I have my share."

"You are about to marry, Jonah—" Reverend Norton firmed his voice "—and while, this time, I would have preferred you to have chosen a wife who would have brought you into the fold of the church so you could worship with us on Sundays, I know how desperately you need a helpmate—and the *right* kind of wife for your circumstances." Reverend Norton inclined his head in Adam's direction. "And he needs a loving mother. Miss Napolitano impresses me. I think she will be very good for both of you."

Jonah set his jaw and nodded.

"The question is...will you be good for her?"

Jonah jerked his head up. "Of course, I will!" Even as he said the emphatic words, doubt slithered through him. He hadn't considered what Lina needed. He didn't even know why a good-looking woman who could have any man had chosen to be a mail-order bride. All he really knew about her was that she was Italian, a good cook, Trudy's friend, and, evidenced by just a little time with Adam, good mother material. That was all that mattered. *Or so I'd thought up until meeting Angelina Napolitano.*

"I think Miss Napolitano, with her Italian blood, will have far more sensibility than your first wife." A smile played about the minister's mouth. "An...emotional, perhaps even *tempestuous,* relationship may be a challenge for you."

Jonah pulled his brows together, not understanding the minister's meaning.

"You will have to give far more of *yourself* in this marriage, Jonah. Your wife will expect more emotion from you...more words. Try to remember your father as he was before your mother died. He was a good husband and obviously loved his wife dearly. *That's* the man, not the one he became, whom you need to emulate."

Jonah's memory of a few minutes ago returned—his father crooking his arm for his mother...the look of tenderness on his face. He swallowed down old sadness. The bitter father that Samuel Barrett became after Ma's death had replaced Jonah's recollection of the loving father.

Jonah met Reverend Norton's gaze. "I'll think on it."

"Good to hear. However, remember that *actions,* not just thoughts, are what will be important."

To Jonah's relief, the sound of the door opening signaled the end of their privacy.

Still wearing his slicker, Seth strode up the aisle, a polished wooden box in his arms. He set the box down on the pew next to Jonah. With an apologetic glance at the minister, he said, "I hope I'm not causing offense, Reverend. I knew Father Fredrick stored his things with Phineas O'Reilly. I stopped by the carpenter's shop to pick this up. I thought if you were inclined, Miss Napolitano could have familiar trappings of her faith, even if she doesn't have Father Fredrick himself."

Reverend Norton stroked his bearded chin, obviously thinking.

Jonah sensed this wasn't an easy decision for the minister.

After a moment, Reverend Norton nodded. "We can use the embroidered altar cloth, swap the cross for the crucifix. We can also set the statue of the Virgin Mary on the altar."

Jonah hoped the ceremonial objects would please Lina. "Thank you for the concessions, sir."

"We Protestants revere Mary as the blessed mother of Jesus. We just don't pray to her." The minister sighed. "Most of my colleagues wouldn't agree with me and, indeed, would condemn my decision to allow—to use an old derogatory term—*papist* trappings in my church."

Jonah had never heard of the word.

"I've long thought the strife between His believers must sadden our Lord. I'm blessed to know Father Fredrick has similar feelings. He and I are old friends. We've had many discussions and debates about doctrine. At the heart of what matters, we believe the same. Jonah, you'll be in good hands with him."

♈

When she'd pictured her marriage, Lina thought she'd feel excited and nervous about marrying Jonah Barrett and starting her new life. She'd tried to imagine his appearance and daydreamed how Adam would react to her. And meeting the child had, indeed, been all she'd hoped for. She fantasized about the look on her bridegroom's face when he saw her in her wedding gown coming up the aisle to him. But she never dreamed she'd feel nervous *and guilty* about the wedding ceremony.

The rain had stopped, thank goodness, and in the distance the clouds opened and let the sun's rays shine golden on the gray mountains—her first glimpse of the beauty of Montana Territory that Trudy had praised in her letter. She climbed the church steps, crossed herself, and sent a silent plea to the Blessed Virgin for strength.

Walking beside her, Trudy gave Lina an anxious glance. "Are you sure about this?*No.* Lina thought of Adam's precious face and stiffened her spine. "I must make the best of this marriage for Adam's sake."

"For your own as well, dear Lina," Trudy said in a gentle voice.

Seth went through the door and stepped inside, holding it open for them.

Trudy reached up to straighten the peony she'd tucked into Lina's hair and pull the lace mantilla over her face. "You look beautiful, and I'm sure Jonah will consider himself lucky in his choice of bride."

I hope so.

"I remember how frightened I was to walk up the aisle. What had seemed like such an adventure in St. Louis was terrifying in reality."

So very true! "If Mr. Barrett and I can find even half the love you and Seth have…"

Seth stuck his head back out the door. "You all right?" He gave Lina a worried glance. "It's not too late to change your mind, come home with us."

Trudy truly has married a good man. "Thank you, Seth." Lina gave them both a steady smile and marched up the steps, determined to get this wedding over with so she could go home with her husband and son and start forging them into a family.

Inside the church, Seth took off his slicker and hung it on a long row of pegs running across the back wall.

A second lower row, for children's apparel, Lina presumed, lined up halfway underneath.

They entered the sanctuary, and she saw the plain wooden room. No scent of incense greeted her. No basin of holy water stood nearby to dip her fingers into. She looked to the front of the church, missing the large crucifix on the wall and the statues of Mary and the saints in niches around the room.

Her stomach tightened. She fastened her gaze on Jonah, standing in front of the altar, with Reverend Norton at his side.

Trudy hurried up the aisle and entered the second pew.

Mrs. Norton began to play an unfamiliar hymn on the piano—one more thing that made Lina feel out of place.

With a reassuring smile, Seth crooked his elbow to her.

As Lina slipped her hand around his arm, her fingers trembled.

Seth briefly covered her hand with his. "Jonah's a good man."

As she took her first steps, Lina glanced at Jonah and realized something else was missing—the rapt expression she'd seen on the face of every bridegroom from the time she was old enough to attend wedding ceremonies. *He should be looking at me with love and expectation and longing.*

But Jonah's face remained impassive, his eyes shadowed.

The lack stabbed her heart, and Lina faltered. *I can't do this.*

Seth glanced down at her and slowed. "Are you all right?" he asked in a low voice.

Lina stared up at him, her body frozen. She couldn't even form words. Only her hand around Seth's arm kept her in place; otherwise she'd whirl and run out of the church.

"Mmma." Adam came into view, moving from behind the front pew.

Seeing the little boy calling to her broke through Lina's paralysis.

Adam smiled at her—not the wide gamin grins she was used to receiving from her nieces and nephews, but enough to lighten his solemn expression. He toddled down the aisle toward her, then held up his hands.

The sight made her heart skip with love. She released Seth's arm, stooped, and opened her arms.

"Mmmm." Adam threw himself at her.

Picking Adam up, Lina held him close, blinking back tears. With the child in her arms, her world steadied. She shifted him to her left hip, and once again tucked her hand around Seth's arm. With a dip of her head toward the front of the church, she indicated her readiness to proceed.

"Good, girl," Seth said, his tone warm.

Lina saw the crucifix and the Madonna on the altar, and a warm glow eased some of the tension in her stomach.

Seth escorted her up the aisle.

This time when she glanced at Jonah, Lina saw him smile, the same small one his son had just given her. *I'll make them both grin,* she vowed. *Our home will be filled with love and laughter!*

After the wedding, the two couples, with Lina carrying Adam, walked outside. Blue patches showed in the cloudy sky, but the street was still awash in mud and puddles.

"I'll go get the wagon," Seth said. "We'll stop at the Norton's to pick up Lina's trunk."

Lina looked up at Jonah. "Is Seth bringing your wagon?"

"I don't have a wagon. Just two horses." One corner of his mouth quirked. "I figured we couldn't fit all your worldly goods into the saddlebags."

She stared up at him, drawn by the glint of humor in his eyes. When he lost his melancholy expression, her husband was a handsome man. A moment passed before what he'd said penetrated her mind. "No wagon? Do you have a buggy? A cart, even?"

Jonah's mouth turned down. "No, ma'am. Koko...my first wife and I rode everywhere. We seldom went to town and had no need for a wagon."

"But, but," she sputtered. "How am I to get around?"

"Koko's mare is very sweet tempered," Jonah said. "I think you'll like her."

Lina wasn't sure whether to feel angry or appalled. "Mr. Barrett, I've never been on a horse in my life!" The words started out sharply but ended with a quiver.

He cut her a worried glance, then looked to Trudy for help.

Lina also turned to her friend.

"I've started riding, Lina," Trudy said. "But then again, I'd ridden before. It had been quite a while, though, since I was in the saddle. The skill came back to me. I'm sure you won't find riding difficult."

Lina's stomach clenched at the thought. *One more thing I didn't take into account! I never even wondered how I'd get around.*

"Didn't you ever want a horse, Lina?"

Lina gave Trudy a rueful smile. "Doesn't every little girl go through a stage of wanting a horse?"

"I remember reading *Black Beauty*, didn't you? I loved that horse."

"We didn't have many books in our family. But one year, our teacher read that story to us in school."

"Well, if it's a black beauty that you want, you'll like Koko's mare. Black with white stockings and a white blaze." Jonah gestured along the length of his nose.

Trudy's reminder of the childhood book settled her stomach somewhat. Lina had forgotten that a horse had once been a girlish dream, intensely longed for, then later supplanted by other interests.

Lina still couldn't stretch her mind around the idea of riding. The thought frightened her. Seeing Seth approach driving the wagon, made Lina decide she had enough problems on the stove in front of her.

I'll shove learning to ride on the back burner.

Chapter Eleven

On the way to the Barrett farm, Trudy and Lina sat in the back of the wagon on a wooden bench padded with a blanket. They'd positioned the bench in the middle of the wagon bed, so their heads didn't touch the wet canvas. The men rode up front on the driver's seat, and Jonah's horse was tied to the back of the wagon. Early in the trip, Adam had fallen asleep in Lina's arms.

The long ride from the church to Lina's new home allowed the two women plenty of time to talk. They reveled in the opportunity to catch up, sharing all the details of their lives since they'd last seen each other.

Lina updated Trudy on the comings and goings at the agency since Trudy had left. Once Trudy had wrung every scrap of information about the other brides from Lina, the conversation turned to Evie. The two women each had different information about Evie—Trudy from Evie's letters and Lina from Mrs. Seymour's trip to Y Knot. Trudy also wanted to know more about Heather's match with Hayden Klinkner.

"Everything looked promising with those two," Lina said. She related Mrs. Seymour's opinion of Hayden and the Klinkner family, then went on to share what Heather had written about Mr. Klinkner's tardy arrival.

"Well, if Mrs. Seymour met him, then I'm sure Heather's all

right. Something probably delayed him, and he showed up right after Heather posted the letter."

Trudy sighed. "Thank goodness, Heather has Evie and Chance, and she's not alone. I won't worry as much knowing she has a friend to turn to. But we must write both Heather and Evie right away so we find out what's happening!"

Their conversation seemed to make the trip fly by. Just as Lina's backside became numb and her limbs were starting to cramp from holding the child, the horses made a turn and came to a stop.

Trudy leaned over and untied the cord holding the canvas at the back closed. She pulled the covering aside. "Oh, good. It's sunny. The ground is terribly muddy though."

"Mud washes off," Lina said in a prosaic tone. "I'm just glad not to get drenched again."

Jonah's face appeared in the opening. "Let me help you, ladies, down." He held out his hand and assisted Trudy out first.

Lina slid over, trying not to awaken the child. She gave Adam to Jonah.

He draped the boy over one shoulder and offered his free hand to Lina.

Hiking her dress up, Lina climbed over the sideboard to the lip of the wagon bed, feeling embarrassed by her awkwardness. She took Jonah's hand and leaned on him to jump down, suddenly aware of his strength. Once she was on the ground, her husband held her hand to make sure she was steady.

"Ready to see your new home?" he murmured, his voice sounding nervous. "It's not as nice as the Flanigans. I know it needs work."

Trudy rolled her eyes. "It's not as nice as the Flanigans is *now*. We've put a lot of elbow grease into the place lately."

Lina studied her new home. As Jonah had written, the house was built with logs and looked sturdy. A long porch punctuated by two windows ran across the front. She glanced over her shoulder to see a view of the mountains, a log barn, pasture and fenced garden, and a large cultivated field.

"You'll enjoy sitting on that porch." Trudy sounded wistful. "The view is so lovely. I'm envious." She shot a glance at her husband.

With a wide grin, Seth held up a hand. "We'll start building you a new porch next week."

Trudy clapped her hands. "Wonderful."

Jonah tilted his head toward the house. "Welcome to my home, Mrs. Barrett. Mr. and Mrs. Flanigan."

As she walked with her hand in Jonah's, Lina picked up her skirt to avoid trailing her hem in the mud. As it was, she'd probably have to soak the bottom in lye overnight to make sure the dirt came out. Careful to avoid puddles, she picked her way across the dirt yard and onto the first step of the porch, where she tried to knock the worst of the mud off her boots. A worn mat of braided straw lay in front of the door, and she scuffed her feet across the open space.

The other three did likewise.

Jonah opened the door and stood back to let her enter.

Light from the windows and the doorway showed her the interior. The room looked spare—a kitchen and main room combination. A ladder led to a loft, which extended half way across the space. A table with peeling white paint and mismatched chairs stood in the middle, separating the kitchen from the living area. One chair had taller legs than the others and was obviously for Adam. A stove, dry sink, icebox, and some open shelves took up the kitchen area.

Two brown leather chairs sat in front of the rock fireplace and set in a row on a deep mantle above the hearth was a row of tattered books, the cloth bindings frayed and faded. So Jonah was a reader, which surprised and pleased her—and explained the clear phrasing of his betrothal letter.

"The layout of this house is very similar to ours," Trudy commented.

"Except ours is stuffed to the gills with the furniture you brought along," Seth said in a teasing voice. "There's probably some to spare that you can give Lina."

Trudy's face lightened. "Excellent idea."

Seth winked at Lina. "Anything to make more room in my barn. My poor animals..." He let out a dramatic sigh.

Everyone laughed.

Jonah waved to a partly open door on the right. "Let me change Adam and lay him down to sleep." He left the main room with the child.

Lina took off her coat. She looked around for someplace to hang the garment.

Trudy pointed to a set of antlers fastened to the wall near the door. "There. We have one similar, but it's a standing hat rack."

Not sure she liked the idea of animal horns as part of the decor, Lina hung up her coat, untied her bonnet strings, pulled off her hat and hung it next to her coat. She stretched out her hands for Seth's coat.

Seth shook his head. "We'll be going. Our hired man will do the milking tonight, but the drive home will still be a long one."

Jonah emerged from the bedroom. "Seth, let's get Lina's trunk from your wagon."

Seth nodded. "I'll help you."

"Don't forget the basket, dear," Trudy called after her husband. "And the pot, valise, and herb box."

"I know you have to be going, but let me prepare you something to eat before you leave." Lina glanced at the almost empty open shelves, then walked over to the cupboard and opened the doors, only to see two cans with no labels, a cloth bag of cornmeal, and a burlap bag of what must be coffee beans, judging by the bitter scent.

Seth trooped in, deposited the herb box and laden pot on the table, and left again.

Trudy looked over her shoulder at the larder. "Oh, dear. Mr. Barrett is in sore need of a wife."

"Good thing I brought some supplies with me. But a trip to town to stock up is certainly in order. Let's see what's in here." Lina looked inside the icebox and saw meat wrapped in waxed paper and a small blue jug, which when she tipped it to see the contents, turned out to be milk. With a flash of chagrin, she wondered what she could serve her guests.

Trudy laid a hand on Lina's arm. "No need. I packed food for us to eat on the way home."

Lina covered Trudy's hand with hers. "I wish you didn't live so far away. You being here made everything better. Once you leave, I'll be on my own." The thought made her chest tighten.

Trudy gave her a rueful glance. "I know all too well what you mean."

Lina lowered her hand. "I'm sure Adam will keep me so busy I won't have time to be lonely." She tried to believe her own words.

"I was so excited about you coming to Sweetwater Springs, Lina, that I didn't stop to think about the distance between us. Or that you didn't ride a horse

"We'll have to become organized about meeting each other."

Trudy paused to think. "We can leave letters at the train station…that's the post office in Sweetwater Springs. On the Sundays Father Fredrick is here, if you come early before mass and meet us after our service, we'll have a chance to visit."

Lina let out a breath in relief. "That helps me feel better."

The men trooped in, each carrying one end of her trunk. They deposited it near the table and left again. When they returned, Jonah had Lina's valise, and Seth the wicker basket, which he held out to his wife.

Trudy took the basket and opened up the white napkin spread over the top. "I baked bread and buttermilk rolls, added a crock of my butter, and made you a dried-apple pie. There's a jar of jam, but it's store-bought. Later when the berries ripen, I intend to make my own."

"How thoughtful of you." Lina set the basket on the table and gave her friend a hug.

From the side of the basket, Trudy took out a little packet of crocheted lace, tied up with a red ribbon.

Lina unfolded the package to reveal two round doilies. She

held them up one at a time, feeling her throat tightened. "Oh, they're just beautiful! I've always admired your handwork."

Trudy beamed with pleasure. "I'm glad you like them."

Jonah came back into the room.

"Look what Trudy made us, Mr. Barrett."

He glanced at the doilies. By his expression, Lina could tell he didn't have any idea what they were. "Pretty," he offered, before moving to Seth's side.

Lina held out her hand to Seth. "Thank you for all you've done for me." She gave Trudy a teasing glance. "I'll be writing a good account of you to Mrs. Seymour and the other brides...Evie as well."

"I've *already* written a good account of him," Trudy playfully protested.

"Yes, but you could have been spreading honey over the truth so as not to worry them," Lina said with a playful smile.

Seth wrapped an arm around his wife's waist and led her to the door. "Make sure you tell them what a handsome fella I am."

The three of them burst out laughing, and even Jonah smiled.

Seth clapped Jonah on the shoulder. "You take care of Lina, hear?"

Jonah cocked one eyebrow. "Else I'll have to answer to you?"

"Worse. You'll have to answer to my wife."

On the wave of their shared laughter, the Flanigans walked out the door.

Lina and Jonah followed and stood on the porch, watching them drive away.

"Will they make it home before dark?" Lina tried not to feel the awkwardness of being left alone with this stranger who was now her husband.

"Probably not. But they'll make it through town and be on the road to the farm before sunset. The horses will know the rest of the way, and there will be enough of a moon to give them some light."

His description made their homes sound so far. Lina stifled a yawn. "Oh, excuse me. I'm so tired.

"You've had a long day."

"But I must unpack. You wouldn't believe everything I've brought with me."

"Besides a pot and a box of plants?" Jonah said, his tone wry.

She chuckled. "The pot was from my mother. She also sent a clay pot, which is wonderful for baking chicken or duckling. The plants are from Nonna, that's grandmother in Italian. The parmesan and provolone cheeses come from my sister Anna and the pasta from Tia Isabella."

As she spoke, Lina removed clothing from the trunk and set the carefully folded piles on the table to reach the kitchen articles underneath. "Tio Vito gave us a sausage maker, and Tio Donaldo and Tio Joseph a bottle of *Chianti* each."

"What's Keeantay?"

"Red wine." Lina reached for a packet of folded oilcloth. "The dried tomatoes came from Tia Nina and the four jars of red sauce from my cousins. Each has her own version, and they have a friendly rivalry about whose is the best. None of the rest of the family will take sides, except their husbands, of course. They don't dare do otherwise."

"You have a big family. And a generous one."

"There's more. The sack of cannellini beans is from Cousin Giovanni. The jar of pickles is from my oldest sister Gina, the jar of strawberry jam is from my other sister Sophia."

"Can't say I've ever had strawberry jam before."

"Never?" She flashed him a quick smile. "You'll love it."

Lina continued placing items on the table. "And there are several kinds of salami and prosciutto." She shrugged. "Too many family members gave them for me to list.

Jonah raised his brows. "Pro...?"

"Prosciutto. It's a delicate ham. Salami's a kind of hard sausage," she explained.

"Ah."

"And then..." Lina tapped a finger against her jaw. "My cousin Josephina made us two pillowcases with crocheted lace on the edges. Tia Angelina and Uncle Antonio insisted I take two of their wine glasses. Tia Anna made me a red-checked tablecloth. Mrs. Hensley, my former employer, gave me a feather bed and cover. That's in the very bottom of the trunk. I'll leave it there for now. Papà built a little toy wagon for Adam."

"I'm surprised you had any room in your trunk."

She laughed. "I wore a uniform for eight years. I don't have many dresses. And I chased after three active boys most of that time. So I never took to wearing a bulky bustle, besides with my best dress, and then only a small cloth one."

"Not many women wear them here. At least, not many that I've seen. Always thought it looked like a ridiculous contraption."

"So do I." They shared a moment of understanding, before Lina rushed to finish the rest of her list. "The string of garlic is from my younger brother, Tonio—'to ward you off if need be,' he told me. Oh, and Tia Maria gave me a rolling pin."

"I guess a rolling pin could also ward me off," Jonah quipped.

She laughed, delighted to hear him making a joke. "Yes. A rolling pin was used on more than dough at Tia Maria and Tio Tony's house. I'll tell the stories to you someday, Mr. Barrett."

"Jonah," he corrected. "We're married now, so call me Jonah."

"*Jonah*, I have enough family stories to tell you one every day for years. But not tonight."

"A story a day. I like that idea."

"Then you shall have it."

Jonah picked up the meat grinder and placed it on a shelf. "Tomorrow, you can organize the kitchen…the whole house, if you'd like." He tilted his head toward the bedroom. "Let me show you where you'll sleep."

Lina scooped up one of the piles of clothes on the table and followed her husband to the bedroom. The room was larger than she expected. A big bed was set against the wall opposite a small window, with a small trundle at the foot.

Adam slept on his back in the middle of the big bed, a pillow on each side. His arms and legs sprawled open, and he looked so sweet that Lina wanted to swoop in and kiss him. But she didn't want to disturb his rest.

A wardrobe stood next to the window. The only other piece of furniture was a small table next to the bed, with a brass candlestick holder, a polished wooden box, and a plain bowl on it. There would be room for her trunk on the other side of the window, and they'd still be able to move around the bed without bashing into anything.

Lina moved closer to the bed, set down her clothes, and touched the covering. "Is this fur?"

"It was my wife's. Uh, Koko's."

She ran her hand over the top. "It must be very warm in the winter. What kind is it?"

Jonah hesitated.

Puzzled, she looked at him, wondering what about her simple question made him stop speaking.

Jonah caught her glance and a corner of his mouth turned up. "Old habit of avoidance. The Blackfoot are very hesitant to use anything of bear origin, or even speak the name of a bear. Unless a man, such as her father was considered protected by bear spirits, then his wife was allowed to prepare a bearskin for the family's use." With a slight smile, he rubbed his hand over the surface. "Koko called this the big bobtail fur. It came from her parents."

Bear spirits? Curious, Lina wanted to know more. "What does the protection consist of?"

"Ferocious bravery in warfare and the power to cure wounds received in action." Pain leaped into his eyes. "But not enough protection to keep a laboring woman from dying."

Lina wanted to take his face in her hands and kiss him—a kiss of comfort. But the gesture, so spontaneous in her demonstrative family, felt too awkward with Jonah, whom she sensed was a reserved man, so she hesitated. *Begin as you mean to go,* she quoted to herself.

Greatly daring, she leaned close, placed her hands on his shoulders, and went on tiptoe to kiss his cheek, her lips brushing over the scratchy beard to land on his cheekbone. "I'm sorry you lost her."

Jonah stepped back, his eyes wide and expression grim. He looked away, the corners of his mouth pulling down.

Lina sucked in a breath. She didn't know if he was reacting to her kiss or if he was missing Koko. But the fact that he moved away gave her a little ache in her heart, even though she told herself such a reaction was to be expected given his circumstances. *Don't give up. He'll come to accept affection...to return affection.*

But what if he doesn't?

Moved by her gesture, Jonah had to resist touching his cheek. The feel of Lina's lips on his face lingered, bringing back a memory of his mother. She'd been fond of kissing him, of kissing his father. He'd forgotten how good affection felt.

Lina placed her hand on Jonah's arm. "Does speaking of Koko cause you pain? Or your baby who died? If it does, we don't need to talk about her."

The compassion in her voice surprised him. Jonah gave her question some thought. "Yes. No. I mean it does cause me pain. But I feel the grief anyway, and..." He gave a slow nod of his head, thinking about the conversation they'd just had. "Sharing with you is good. If you don't mind that is."

She gave him an encouraging smile, although her eyes looked sad.

"The baby was a girl. She..." His breath caught. "She looked just like Adam when he was born. So tiny." Jonah cleared his throat. "Now, she lies in her mother's arms. I like to imagine them together."

"That is a beautiful thought." Lina squeezed his arm. "I want to learn about Koko. She was your wife...Adam's mother. I want you to feel you can speak freely. And...we need to keep her memory alive for Adam's sake."

Her generosity of spirit moved him. Jonah didn't know that much about women, but he suspected many would not like hearing about a first wife, especially an Indian wife. They'd be trying to brush Koko's existence under the rug. But he didn't know how to put his appreciative feelings into words.

To change the subject, Jonah strode to the wardrobe. He patted the side. "There's plenty of room in here for your dresses."

"It's a beautiful piece." Lina moved closer. "The carvings look very unusual. I'll have to examine them closer in the morning light."

"Gideon Walker made it. He's our nearest neighbor and likes to build furniture."

"I'll look forward to meeting him."

"Might be a while. He's pretty much a hermit. We'd talked about Gid making a headboard and chest of drawers to match." Jonah had a sudden image of Lina in the bed with him, their naked bodies entwined. Guilt made him shove away the image. He edged toward the door, avoiding looking at his bed.

"Ah…Seth mentioned he slept in the loft at his place and let Trudy have the bed. So I think I'll do the same. But Adam sleeps with me." He gestured toward the bed. "He'd just started sleeping alone because of the new baby coming and all, when…" He exhaled a ragged breath. "Then after Koko died…" He shrugged. "Guess we both needed the comfort."

"If you don't mind, Adam can sleep with me."

Jonah ran a hand through his hair. "Just until he becomes used to you. Then we can move him to the trundle. For now, I'll make a pallet in front of the fire so I can be close if either of you needs me."

Lina leaned over and touched Adam's bare foot. His flannel nightshirt had crept up to his waist, exposing an odd wrapping around his bottom. "What's he wearing?"

"The rabbit skin wraps with moss inside. The moss is in the box here." He tapped the box on the side table. "Bear grease in this one."

"Moss? Bear grease?" Her eyebrows pulled together.

"For his bottom." Jonah didn't understand her puzzlement. He reached over to the table, dipped his hand in the box, pulled out a clump of moss, and held it up for her inspection.

"You use *moss* on his bottom?"

He winced at the incredulous tone in her voice. "What else could you possibly use?"

"Cloth diapers and soakers."

Now it was his turn to be puzzled. "Soakers?"

"Tightly knitted pants. The cloth diaper goes inside for when he soils himself."

Jonah rocked back on his heels. "Ah, I see the problem. We are talking about Indian ways versus white ways. I never had anything to do with babies before Adam, so I wouldn't know the difference."

Lina's shoulders relaxed. "I'm glad we figured out why we were at cross purposes." She held out her hand. "May I see the moss?"

He dropped the clump into her palm.

She held it to her nose.

He knew the moss gave off a grass-and-earth scent, not unpleasant.

With her free hand, Lina spread out the rabbit skin and fingered the ties at the edges. "Well, at least you don't have to wash diapers this way."

"Adam uses the pot or the outhouse outside, around the right corner of the house. If I'm not here, stand him in front of it first thing in the morning and make a *ssss* noise. That's his signal to go. And if he makes that noise, you'll know what it means."

She made a wry sound. "I suspect you and I will go round in circles a few more times until we settle in."

He ran a hand through his hair. "I 'spect so."

"Well." Lina smiled and shrugged. "We have much to learn about each other's ways."

"That we do." But as he said the words, Jonah couldn't help

feeling ashamed about his lack of knowledge. A normal man would have grown up around siblings and babies and know more about women and the kinds of things people learn in school and church. Not just about book learning, but about people learning. Koko had accepted him for who he was and didn't expect him to be different. But would Lina?

Chapter Twelve

The room was still dark when Lina woke, the temperature cool but pleasant. She sensed dawn wasn't far away.

Adam slept at her side, his body warm and heavy. During the night, she'd felt some arm jabs or kicks when he shifted, but she'd been so tired, the movements barely registered.

She groped for the candle on the nightstand and the matchbox she'd set next to it. She struck the match and lit the wick. Then she placed the glass chimney over the candle. In the light of the flame, she glanced at the watch she'd left next to the candlestick, a Christmas gift one year from the Hensleys. Half past five.

Lina eased out of bed and used the chamber pot set into a small seat and tucked under the bed. She'd empty it later when there was more light. She dressed and braided her hair, twisting the plait into a bun and stabbing in hairpins. Bringing the candlestick with her, she walked into the other room, trying to move silently, and went to the basin in the kitchen area to wash her hands and face.

Once she'd dried off with a towel, Lina lit the oil lamp on the table, making a mental note to clean the glass before the evening. The candle and the lamp provided enough illumination to work in the kitchen.

Carrying the lamp, Lina tiptoed to the other side of the room to check on Jonah. Her husband lay with his face turned toward her, one muscled arm out of the blanket, and she wondered how long it would be before the two of them developed a feeling of intimacy and were comfortable sharing the bed.

Soon, I hope. She wanted to experience for herself the passion between husband and wife, hinted at during conversations between the women of her family, or seen in a hearty kiss or pinch of a bottom, or heard in the night noises behind a closed door. And she wanted to make a baby.

Returning to the kitchen area, Lina opened the stove door and saw Jonah had left the interior clean of ashes and had set out larger logs and kindling over what looked like pine cones and dried moss instead of the crumbled newspaper she was used to. Blessing him for his thoughtfulness, she adjusted the damper. Then she picked up a tin near the stove, lifted the top to find matches inside, and lit the fire.

Taking her enamel pot, she tiptoed to the door to go outside to pump some water. No Italian kitchen was complete without minestrone simmering on the stove. Her first task as a new wife was to begin making the soup. Then she'd figure out what to serve her husband and son for breakfast.

❧

A rich aroma, savory and unfamiliar, along with the sound of humming, pulled Jonah from a deep sleep—the most refreshing rest he'd had in weeks. For a few minutes, he lay still, noting the gray dawn casting faint gleams into the darkened room, lit only by an oil lamp and a candle in the kitchen area. Drowsy, he watched his new wife stand at the stove, her curvy figure wrapped in shadows.

Lina looked out the window, and from her profile, he saw the half curve of a smile. Then she lifted an arm and dropped something into the kettle she'd brought, making stirring motions.

I need to get up and milk the cow. But Jonah allowed himself another few minutes to remain on his pallet. Since Koko's death, he hadn't experienced any moments of peace and had almost forgotten the feeling of relaxation. The shadows in the room gradually lightened.

He took a deep inhale, then exhaled and sat up. "Good morning."

Lina tossed him a quick smile over her shoulder and gave the pot another stir. "*Buongiorno*, sleepy one."

Jonah saw she held a wooden spoon and wondered what she was making that smelled so wonderful.

Lina waved her wooden spoon at him, giving him encouragement. "Say it. *Buongiorno*."

He tried to make his mouth form the unfamiliar word. "*Buuongorno*."

She chuckled. "Close enough."

The sound of her throaty laughter energized him. Jonah threw back the bearskin covering and stretched his arms.

Lina quickly looked away, studying the interior of the pot.

In the faint light, Jonah couldn't tell if his wife was blushing, but he thought she might be. He pulled on his pants, tucking his nightshirt inside the waist and settling the suspenders over his shoulders. He'd change his shirt later.

Curious, he followed the enticing smell over to the stove. Steam rose from the pot. He peered inside at the boiling reddish liquid. "Are you making soup?"

"*Soup?* Lina repeated the word as if offended. "Not just soup. This is *minestrone!*"

The passion in her voice amused him. "Minestrone?"

"Yes, minestrone." She gestured with the wooden spoon. "In a village outside of Rome, my nonna learned to make it from her nonna, and she from hers…"

"A very old recipe."

"There is no recipe. Minestrone is made from whatever meat, spices, and vegetables are at hand. When times are well, the soup is thick with meat, usually pork but sometimes beef, and vegetables. When times are lean, so is the soup. But not today. I brought pasta noodles with me. Garlic, dried tomatoes..." She waved at the icebox. "I found some meat in there, although I didn't recognize it."

"Venison."

"Oh, a deer," Lina's voice trailed off. Then she visibly perked up. "Well, that will certainly be something to write home to Nonna about. I know she's never made venison minestrone. I wonder if the taste will be as good as beef broth?"

"Your broth should actually be richer tasting with the venison than with beef. I think you'll like it. Venison makes good broth, although it's not as fatty as beef."

"Something new for both of us, then. Minestrone for you and venison for me."

"What is pasta?"

Lina stared slack-jawed at Jonah. "Noodles." Her teeth worried at her lower lip. "I never imagined someone not knowing about pasta." Her voice was slow and thin. "That you have to ask...makes me realize how far I am from home."

Not knowing what to do about her homesickness, he stayed on the topic of minestrone. "Like Mrs. Norton had in the soup she served us yesterday."

"Mrs. Norton's noodles were different. I suspect she dropped some kind of batter into the soup. Pasta is made beforehand in a uniform size and air-dried."

He shook his head, not understanding.

"Here, let me show you." Lina reached for a burlap bag on the table, scooped up a handful, and opened her palm to display the pasta. "*Macaroni.*"

"They look like something you wear."

She smiled. "As girls, my sisters, cousins, and I would string necklaces and bracelets with them. We felt like princesses with our jewelry." With a flick of her wrist, she tossed them in the pot. "You'll see. They're good to eat."

"If you say so."

"You wait. I think you'll like it. *And* to listen to my nonna...Minestrone makes you strong and healthy as well as cures all sorts of ills...headaches, colds, indigestion, gout, liver ailments, and even heartaches..." She faltered and looked at Jonah, an apology showing in her eyes. "Well, perhaps not *cures* heartaches." She gave him a timid smile. "But I think you'll find minestrone to be a comforting meal."

Her words brought back his sense of loss. *More than a meal is needed to comfort me.* Jonah tilted his head to the door. "I'm going to go milk the cow."

"What do you eat for breakfast?"

"Porridge or cornmeal mush."

She made a tisking sound. "That sounds fine for Adam but not enough for a hard-working man. Do you have chickens for eggs? Bacon or ham?"

"No chickens or pigs. Had a pig before. But a bear got him. I shot the bear though, so we evened out. There's not much call to go to town." He shrugged. "We usually eat wild game—deer or elk, goose, turkey... I'll be fine with soup."

She drew herself up as if offended. "The minestrone won't be ready until later. But I'll figure out something. You need to start the day with a good breakfast."

Jonah couldn't help but smile at her ruffled feathers. "Yes, ma'am. I'll be off to milk the cow to get you started."

"After breakfast, can you go to town for supplies? I can give you a list of what we need."

Go to town again? Jonah rarely went into Sweetwater Springs for supplies. Being in town made him uncomfortable—too many unfriendly people. The forests and the land supplied most of what his family needed. But he could hardly deny his bride's request. "You make up a list of what you need. I'll ride into town in a few days. Now that you're here to watch Adam, I have chores I need to catch up on first."

"A few days?" Lina said in a sharp tone. "We'll need supplies before then."

"I'll go hunting. It's not the best time of year, but there's still game to be had."

"Hunting?" Her tone didn't soften. "Whatever will you hunt?"

He shrugged. "Squirrel, rabbit…maybe a turkey." Jonah didn't mention that he really planned on a deer. He wanted to surprise Lina with a buck. With luck, a couple of days of hunting would provide meat for several weeks.

"Squirrel?" Lina said in a faint voice. "What do you do with a squirrel?"

"Fry it up," Jonah said in a matter-of-fact tone. "Spit-roast or stew with root vegetables. Although—" he was struck by an old memory "—my ma used to make squirrel pie. Mighty tasty."

Lina put her hands on her hips. "Jonah Barrett, to make a pie of any kind, I'll need flour, butter, eggs…"

Surprised by the passion of her response, he held up a hand to stem the flow of words. "I believe Ma's old churn is in the barn."

"In the barn?" Lina echoed, drawing her black brows together. "Didn't Koko ever use it?"

Jonah shook his head. "We didn't have a cow then. Bought it after she died so Adam could have the milk."

"I've never made butter before."

"Neither have I." He shifted his weight, anxious to get started on the day's tasks. "I remember my ma working hard at it, though."

She lowered her arms. "One of my aunts made the butter for our whole family. When I was a girl, I helped her a few times. I guess I can figure it out."

"I have no doubt you will."

A pleased smile crossed her face.

The problem of going to town headed off at the pass. "But before you make butter, I have to milk the cow." He couldn't resist teasing his city-bred wife. "Unless you want to do it."

Lina rolled her eyes. "I've never milked a cow in my life."

"I'll teach you sometime." Jonah reached for the milk pail sitting on the shelf next to the icebox, tilted his head toward the door, and left the house. As he walked to the barn thinking about his bride, Jonah became aware of an unusual spring in his step, of the way he was swinging the empty milk pail. *So far, everything seems to be working out with my mail-order bride.*

♡

About an hour later, after a breakfast of cornmeal mush and milk for Adam and slices of salami and cheese on buttered bread for him and Lina, Jonah prepared to leave the house for the day's hunting. He took down the rifle from the rack over the door and grabbed the pouch with the bullets that hung beside it.

As she wiped Adam's face and hands and set him on the floor, Lina kept glancing at Jonah through lowered eyelashes, as if she expected something from him.

He couldn't figure out what his wife wanted. Feeling awkward, as if he'd just missed something important, Jonah gave her a little salute good-bye. Then he strode over to Adam sitting on the floor with his toys, both the new ones from Lina and the small leather ball he'd already had, and ruffled the boy's hair. "You be good for your new ma, hear?"

The boy looked up. His expression remained solemn.

"Stay safe, Jonah," Lina said, her voice firm as though she was giving him a command.

"Of course." He nodded good-bye. Carrying his rifle, he hurried to the barn. There, Jonah changed out of his clothes and put on a buckskin shirt and pants that were stiff with dried blood from earlier hunting trips. He strapped the belt holding his long knife around his waist and looped the worn leather strap of the battered canteen that his father had carried in the Civil War over his shoulder. Picking up a burlap sack he'd previously filled with a mixture of alfalfa and dried huckleberry vines, Jonah slung the strap over his other shoulder.

He walked out of the barn and moved around the field that he still needed to finish planting—his next task after he'd brought in enough game—and headed toward the forest. As he entered the canopy of the trees, he stayed alert to his surroundings, cataloging the sights and sounds around him, and inhaling the woodsy scent of leaves.

Jonah hiked along a familiar trail, avoiding sticks that would snap under his feet. He couldn't move through the woods as stealthily as Koko's brothers, but certainly more silently than the few white men he'd hunted with.

In the distance, a wild turkey called. Jonah debated about veering from his plan, then decided to continue to the small meadow he'd set up to lure deer. He hadn't been there for weeks, but hopefully, the alfalfa he carried would entice the deer to appear.

Swinging along the trail, Jonah became conscious of a freedom to his movements—how his soul soaked up the solitude and beauty of the wilderness, and his pulse quickened as he imagined a good hunt. Grateful thoughts of Lina intruded, and he wondered how she was faring with Adam. Because of his marriage and Lina's care for him and his son, his body felt lighter, his mind more relaxed and focused than any time since Koko and the babe's death.

Even the reminder of Adam's mother didn't bring the usual pain, for Jonah sensed her presence at his side, almost as if she strode with him, strong and silent, her mane of black hair fluttering in the breeze. The company of his two wives, Lina in his mind and Koko in spirit, beside him, felt comforting and right. Jonah imagined the three of them as a team—if you could see three horses pulling a wagon, instead of the usual one or two pair—with Adam riding along, smiling and happy.

At the meadow, Jonah dismissed his fanciful thoughts, focusing on spreading the huckleberry vines and alfalfa where he'd have a good shot. Then he climbed into a tree, settled himself in a comfortable fork that gave him a good view, and leaned against the trunk, preparing to wait.

Chapter Thirteen

All during breakfast, Lina waited for Jonah to comment on the food. She doubted if he'd ever eaten salami and provolone cheese on buttered bread before and wondered what he thought of the open-faced sandwiches she'd made. She had to guess from how his eyes widened at his first taste, the thoughtful way he chewed, and the slight nod after he finished his first bite.

He was quiet throughout the meal.

Lina made up for his silence by chattering about the mail-order bridal agency and telling him about her friend Heather. "I'm so worried about her. As soon as I have a chance, I'm going to write a letter to Y Knot."

"Y Knot?" Jonah wrinkled his forehead. "Can't say I've heard of it. Do you know where the town is situated?"

"I looked at Mrs. Seymour's map. More south of here. Heather had to take the stagecoach from the train."

Lina finished her breakfast, her mind on Heather's dilemma. *How frustrating to be kept from lighting a candle in a church and saying a special prayer for her that all will be well!*

I can pray for her anywhere and any time, Lina reminded herself. But she missed the comfort of the ritual.

After they'd finished, when Jonah left to hunt with just a touch of a finger to his forehead in a salute, Lina couldn't stop a feeling of disappointment. She'd hoped for a good-bye kiss. Her father and uncles always gave their wives a hug or hearty buss on the lips or cheeks, and perhaps even a pat on the fanny when they left for the day. *Will he always be so reserved with me?*

Feeling lonely and homesick, Lina picked up Adam and carried him out to the porch, taking a seat on the bench. The breakfast dishes could wait. She just wanted to hold her son. At least, he was affectionate, and she wanted to enjoy every minute with him.

Adam seemed to still be sleepy and for a while lay back with his head on her chest. The feel of her child and the beauty of the brilliant blue sky over the mountains calmed her troubled spirits.

When the boy wiggled to get down, Lina briskly told herself to don a more cheerful outlook and to start work around the house.

A few hours later, after being on her own with a toddler all morning, Lina realized being a mother was no easy task, and she'd discovered a new appreciation for her family. She'd resented the abundance of relatives—the way they practically lived on top of each other—how she could sneeze and a cousin three doors down would say, "*salute!*" Their nosiness, with everyone knowing each other's business, had annoyed her. The ever-increasing noise level, whenever two or more of them gathered together, made her long for the quiet of solitude.

Be careful what you wish for.

Even though her family teemed with babies and toddlers, there were always plenty of arms to hold a fussy baby when a beleaguered mother needed a break. Even the younger children were good at playing with the little ones.

Lina could recall, when she was twelve, Tia Isabella wearily trooping into their house, depositing baby Joey in her arms, and saying, "Take him before I drop him in the rain barrel." Then, with an air of dusting off her hands, her aunt marched back out the door. Lina had been proud of her ability to soothe fractious Joey, and her mother and grandmother had praised her skill with babies.

Now, she had no one and couldn't get to all the work of unpacking and organizing the house because Adam constantly wanted her attention. At first, Lina reveled in holding and rocking him. She tried to coax him to say Italian words and showered kisses on his cheeks and forehead. A few times she blew noisily on his stomach to make him squirm and smile.

But after a while, the need to work tugged at her conscience. While Lina wouldn't say the cabin was filthy, the house certainly didn't live up to her standards. And, although the plants she'd brought would probably be fine for a few days in the box, she was eager to get started on her garden. Then there was the butter she wanted to make.

When Lina stood Adam on the floor, he started to fuss, making "mmmma" noises and holding out his hands. So, of course, she picked him up. She tried distracting him with the toy wagon and the tin soldiers she'd bought for him. He stared at the toys but made no move to play with them, so she sat next to him and demonstrated how the wagon rolled when pushed or marched a soldier across the floor and into the wagon.

He gave her his small smile and reached for a soldier.

Relieved, Lina rose, only to have him protest. She played some more, then tried giving him a spoon to bang on a pot. Adam was fine as long as she sat next to him, but as soon as she moved away, he objected.

For a little while she was able to hold him on her hip and use one hand to take dishes off the shelves and stack them on the table, but he soon became too heavy. Not for the first time, Lina wondered why God hadn't made women with four arms—two to hold a baby and two to work with.

Exhausted, she lay down with Adam to get him to take a nap and fell asleep as well, waking only when he kicked her hip. As much as she longed to keep napping, Lina knew she needed to use the time to work around the house. Easing out of bed, she tiptoed from the room grateful the boy appeared to be a deep sleeper.

Once in the main room, she looked around, debating where

to begin. The familiar smell of the minestrone, wafting from the pot simmering on the stove and making the house smell like home, comforted her. She debated about gardening, then decided she didn't want to go out of earshot of Adam. Lina decided to clean and arrange the house, then make a list of everything she needed.

She started with the cupboard, then tackled the open shelves, moving mismatched dishes, glasses, silverware, cooking utensils, a jar of some kind of grease, and a tin of willowbark tea to the table. The more Lina explored the paltry contents of Jonah's kitchen, the more she wondered how he'd managed to keep himself and Adam fed. On one hand, she was irritated by the lack of food and ingredients, of not having the kitchen tools, pots, and pans she was used to working with. On the other hand, the meager state of the kitchen supplies made her realize how much Jonah and Adam needed her.

For a while, the thought sustained her. Lina hummed as she worked, content to be busy, to be setting her new home to rights. Her thoughts dwelt on her husband, on the hint of melancholy in his green eyes when he didn't realize she was looking at him.

What would it be like to see Jonah smile, to see his eyes alight with joy…with tenderness?

For as much as she took pleasure in being needed, Lina knew she also longed to be loved. *How long will it take?*

Lina had never been a naturally patient person. She'd carefully cultivated what patience she possessed through working as a nanny. An employee in a prestigious household had certain responsibilities and obligations, or that person was replaced. *Somehow, I'll have to school myself to wait in this situation as well.*

Once the shelves were clean, Lina took pride in arranging the items she'd brought with her. The bags of pasta went into the cupboard along with the sacks of cornmeal and coffee and the two cans. She made a mental note to ask Jonah about their contents, and then set the jar of grease and tin of willowbark tea next to the cans.

On the shelves, the jars of sauce and pickles gleamed red and green next to a long rectangular tin of spaghetti noodles, standing upright next to the two bottles of Chianti. Lina hung the string of garlic from a nail near the side of the cupboard. She placed two halves of the clay pot together on a shelf next to the meat grinder; then came a basin, a roasting pan, a cake rack, and other pans, a short stack of tin plates, tin cups, the two wine glasses, and an enamel speckled coffeepot. She'd filled an old Mason glass jar with wooden spoons and other cooking utensils and placed it within reach of the stove.

She'd swept the floor—an arduous task with the broom made of twigs tied together rather than straw—laboring with four strokes to the normal one. After tossing the debris over the porch railing, she spread the red-and-white checked tablecloth over the table, where the clean glass of the lamp sparkled in the sunshine streaming through the now-clear kitchen window.

When Lina finished, she stepped back, pleased with her efforts. She imagined what the shelves would look like when they were full of supplies and daydreamed of all of the meals she'd prepare for her family. Someday, she'd have daughters helping her cook and bake. She pictured a laden table, a row of cherubic faces on both sides, with each child having Jonah's green eyes.

A noise from the bedroom made her whirl and hurry to check on Adam.

He shifted positions, opened his eyes, and then closed them again.

Quietly, Lina took a pen, ink, and paper—a gift from Mrs. Seymour—from her trunk and returned to the main room, where she sat at the table and started a list of what they needed from town. When she finished, she wrote a note to her family to let them know she'd arrived safely. By mentioning the Madonna on the altar in the church, Lina was able to imply she was married in a Catholic ceremony without actually telling her family a lie. She described Jonah and Adam and the house, making sure to detail what she'd done with each gift from her family. Then she requested some flannel to make diapers and two pairs of soakers for Adam.

Before she could write further requests or begin a letter to Heather, Adam made a sound, and Lina went to get him.

When the boy saw her, he smiled and held out his hands.

"Ah, *carissimo!*" Her heart full of love, she picked up Adam and hugged him to her, kissing his face.

After making sure he'd used the pot, she took him outside, where they searched for wildflowers to make a bouquet for the table. She sent quick glances toward the forest. *Is Jonah on his way home? Was his hunt successful?*

Lina suppressed a shiver. *Remember to act pleased when he hands over the meat,* she instructed herself. *Pretend it's a slab of bacon. After all, bacon was once a pig. I've witnessed pig slaughtering before.* She shuddered, remembering how her brothers had teased her about her squeamishness, and vowed not to let Jonah down with feminine weakness.

Back inside the house, she artfully arranged the wild flowers in a blue-colored Mason jar. Finished with the kitchen, Lina started on the bedroom so she could unpack and put away her clothes while Adam sat on the bed, a tin soldier clutched in each hand.

As the sun started to drop toward the horizon, with rising apprehension, Lina frequently stepped onto the porch to watch for Jonah's return. She hadn't expected him to be gone all day. After all, how long did shooting some squirrels take? She'd seen a couple frisking in the trees on the edge of the fields.

As the shadows lengthened, her mind conjured visions of what could have detained him. Maybe he'd tripped and fallen, breaking his leg. Or maybe he'd been attacked by a bear or a lion. *Are there lions in Montana Territory?*

Her fears tumbled over each other like pebbles in the swift-moving stream she'd seen on the Hensley's country estate. *What will I do if something has happened to Jonah? How will I find him? And if he doesn't return, where will I go for help?* With dismay, Lina realized she didn't even know the way to town, or to the Flanigans. She pressed a hand to her chest to calm her racing heart.

The beginnings of dusk cast misty silver across the blue sky, muting the sun, and tingeing the feathery clouds pink and gold. Jonah tromped home in triumph with the heavy body of the white-tailed deer hanging over his shoulders, the weight of the animal slowing his steps. Although he'd washed up in the creek that ran through the meadow, he knew the gutted, headless carcass still dripped over his blood-stained clothes.

Energy charged through him. Anxious to present Lina with the deer, Jonah didn't bother to move silently down the path. His wife would soon see he could provide for his family, so there was no need to rush to town.

As much as he'd needed the solitude of the forest—the chance to go into the wilderness without the encumbrance of a little boy—he missed Adam. Since Koko's death, he hadn't been away from his son for more than a few minutes. In the past, Jonah had always been eager to return to the house from his hunts, but not like this. Now he felt as if a fishing line had hooked to his gut and was yanking him home.

Jonah kept picturing the proud look on Lina's face when she saw his kill and wondered what strange Italian dishes she'd prepare with the venison.

At noon, he'd eaten a sandwich made up of cheese and a different kind of sausage from breakfast, spicy enough to make him grateful for the canteen of water he'd brought along. He'd never tasted anything like the food Lina had prepared for him— foreign and flavorful—an unexpected windfall in acquiring his Italian mail-order bride.

He was almost at the house when his wife stepped out on the porch. Jonah smiled at her, straightening his shoulders, as much as possible beneath a heavy carcass, so she could see what he'd brought her.

Lina screamed and raced toward him, her dark eyes wide.

She came to a sudden halt, scanned him, let out a shriek, and threw up her hands to cover her face. Turning on her heel, she ran the other direction and into the house.

Ears ringing, Jonah stared after her, his thoughts befuddled. *Did I marry an insane woman and leave her to care for my son?* With hurried strides, he followed, needing to make sure of Adam's safety.

Before he'd gone many steps, Adam appeared in the doorway and greeted him with a smile that went a long way to settling Jonah's fear for his son, even if his concerns about his wife didn't ease.

Jonah glanced down at himself and grimaced. He didn't want to track blood into the house, so he waved at the boy, turned, and headed to the skinning shed tacked on behind the barn.

How had everything gone so wrong? Koko had never behaved that way.

At the thought of his deceased wife, his steps slowed. Koko would have greeted his return with a wide smile of pride and gotten right to skinning the deer. Jonah had no doubt his new wife was proficient with a knife when it came to chopping vegetables, but that dressing-out a deer was not among her homemaking gifts.

Jonah figured he'd better resign himself to doing his own skinning.

Chapter Fourteen

Lina raced across the yard, up the porch, and into the house. Her momentum carried her almost into the table, and she braced her hands on the surface, gasping for air, shaking, and trying to blink away the vision of Jonah covered in blood. *Madonna mia!* Her heart still thumped hard enough to plunge out of her skin, and her stomach quivered with nausea. To see her husband drenched in blood, to think he'd been mortally wounded, and then to realize the source, the headless animal draped over his shoulders—it was a shock!

She crossed herself. *Madonna mia, I can't do this! I can't live a frontier life. I thought I could, but I can't.*

But the cry of Adam, who stared at her, checked her runaway thoughts. Feeling guilty for her weak sensibilities and for frightening the boy, Lina hurried to pick him up. Still upset, she kissed his forehead and pressed him to her heart. Once again, Lina realized that she could never leave this child.

The blood-soaked carcass of the deer jumped back into her memory. *O Signore, this just won't do. Think of Francesco Marconi's butcher shop, of the meat hanging from hooks in the ceiling. This is the same thing. Women out here must cope with bloody kills all the time, even Trudy. Surely, Seth hunted too. Koko must have been an expert in dealing with game.*

At the thought of Jonah's first wife, shame clenched Lina's

stomach into a knot. As an Indian, Koko probably accepted bloody game as a matter of course. Maybe she even hunted with him. She remembered the shocked look on Jonah's face. *He probably thinks I've taken leave of my senses!*

While Lina regretted her undue reaction, her heart still raced, and her breathing was rapid. She pulled out a chair and sat for a minute, feeling shaky. The weight of Adam on her lap steadied her. But all too soon, he wiggled to be set down, then toddled to the door, forcing her to follow him.

Once on the porch, Lina gave a furtive glance around but saw no sign of Jonah or the deer and sank down onto the bench.

Adam handed her a toy soldier, then picked up a second and gave her that one as well. For a few minutes, Lina played with him, then realized she needed to get supper on the table and carried him back into the house.

Lina added some sticks to the fire to bring the minestrone to a boil. The men in her family liked their soup piping hot, and she figured Jonah would to. She dipped in the long-handled strainer and ladled out some noodles, which she dropped into a bowl to cool for Adam.

She took down the wine glasses and uncorked a bottle of Chianti, pouring some into a glass. Lina sipped the wine while she set the table and placed Trudy's basket of rolls and the crock of butter near the vase of wild flowers, which she'd centered on the doily.

Tomorrow will be a better day. I'll make pasta and red sauce, and all will be well.

Just as she finished, Jonah walked in. He'd changed his clothes, and the hair around his face was damp, showing he'd splashed water on his face.

Relieved he wasn't still bloody, Lina gave him a cheerful smile, pretending she hadn't just run away from him screaming.

He eyed her warily.

Adam toddled over to his father. "Pa, pa."

Jonah picked the boy up for a hug, his gaze on her the whole time.

Perhaps, I shouldn't pretend nothing is wrong. "I'm sorry for my...reaction. When I saw all the blood, I thought you were hurt."

"I was *hunting*, Lina. That does tend to make a man bloody." He set down Adam, and the boy clung to his leg.

His sarcasm sparked her heated nerves. "You said s*quirrels*, Jonah," she snapped. "That's what I was prepared for. Not—" Lina waved her hands in the air, indicating something big. "After you were gone all day, I became worried, thinking something might have happened to you." Her voice quivered, and she made a limp-wristed gesture toward the forest. "Out there."

He spread out his fingers. "I wanted to surprise you with a deer."

"Oh, you certainly surprised me!"

Jonah threw his arms out in evident frustration. "I thought you'd be *pleased*. I brought home a lot of meat. We'll have steaks and can make jerky."

"Jerky?" Provoked, she, too, waved her arms. "What is this *jerky*?"

"Dried meat strips. Lasts a long time. We'll store some for the winter."

"I don't know how to make jerky!"

"I'll show you."

Lina jammed her fists into her waist in defiance. "I'll make sausages."

"I don't know how to make sausages," Jonah echoed her.

Is he mocking me? "I'll show you," she said, imitating his words and tone.

"That's fine. I don't mind learning."

"But I don't know the cuts of meat to use. It's not like a pig. I know my way around a pig's body." She shrugged. "We don't have casings for the sausage anyway." After taking a breath, she modulated her tone. "So I guess it will have to be sausage patties and jerky then."

"Jerky is good to have on hand," he said, sounding relieved.

"Keeps a long time. I can take it with me when I hunt without worrying if the meat will spoil."

"I'll learn to make your jerky, Jonah."

He dipped his chin and gave her a small smile. "You can do both."

Lina lowered her arms, feeling glad they had come to a compromise after their first tiff.

॰

Lina's panic was foreign to Jonah and concerned him. Her explanation somewhat relieved his mind. *I must give her time to adjust to a rougher way of living and not judge her too harshly.*

She placed a bowl on the table in front of Adam's high chair and set a small spoon she must have brought from St. Louis next to it.

Jonah was touched that she'd thought of his son's need before even meeting him. He glanced at the wooden cart. Apparently her family had thought of Adam too.

He watched the lamplight warm Lina's rose-tinted cheeks and longed to cup her chin in his hand. *Odd thought.* With Koko their relationship had been a partnership. *With Lina will it be more? But I don't want more, do I?*

Striving to simply enjoy her company, Jonah put away dour thoughts and picked up his son, nuzzling his dark hair. He positioned Adam in the high chair and pushed it close to the table.

His son ignored the spoon and reached into the bowl, picking up a noodle and putting it in his mouth. He must have liked the taste, for he reached for two handfuls, shoving in the morsels with both fists.

Lina didn't seem to mind. She gave Adam an indulgent smile. "Perhaps we'll introduce him to the spoon another time when he's more familiar with pasta." She handed him what amounted to a peace offering—a glass of the dark red wine. "For our first supper."

He accepted the glass. "I've never had wine. Whisky. But not wine."

"In my family, that would be a sacrilege. Italians have wine, not blood, running through their veins."

He chuckled.

"*Salute.*" Lina made a little flourish with her glass and clinked it against his. "That means health." She sipped.

Jonah followed her example. The taste of the wine reminded him a bit of tart cherries although smokier. He wasn't sure if he liked the flavor, but thought he could become used to drinking wine.

They each took a seat at opposite ends of the table.

Jonah reached for a roll, buttered the piece, and raised it to his mouth.

"Let us pray," Lina said.

Embarrassed, Jonah lowered his arm.

Hands clasped in front of her, she stared at him for a moment. "Allow me. My family says this prayer in Italian. Then I'll repeat it in English."

"Very well." He folded his hands together and bowed his head, remembering saying grace with his parents.

"Dio, benedisci il cibo sulla tavola e dai da mangiare a quelli che non ce l'hanno. Dio, ti ringrazio per il pane quotidiano e benedisci la nostra tavola. Dio, ti ringrazio per il cibo che ci dai."

Jonah liked the melodic flow of Lina's words.

"Lord, bless the food on the table and feed those who have none. Lord, thank you for our daily bread and bless our table. Lord, thank you for the food you have given us."

"Thank you, Lina." Her bright smile warmed his insides.

"This minestrone isn't my best," she said, her cheeks deepening in hue. "All I had were dried tomatoes, spices, pasta, garlic, and venison."

He scooped up a spoonful of the fragrant minestrone and tasted it, enjoying the rich flavor. *If this isn't her best, I look forward to future bowls of soup.*

For a while they ate in silence, and Jonah savored each

spoonful. After Lina served Jonah his second bowl, he slowed his pace. He glanced around the room, noting the changes he'd been too worried to see before. He fingered a red square on the tablecloth and noticed the jar of wildflowers. Lina had also cleaned the glass chimney of the lamp. The shelves in the kitchen held more items. She must have a magic trunk to have stored so much inside.

"The place looks…like a home," he said.

"Thank you. I had time when Adam slept."

Jonah brought his gaze back to hers. "You were going to tell me a story, remember."

"That's right." Lina set down her spoon. "Which story to choose," she mused. "I'll start with an old country story. Before they came to America, my grandparents had a small farm, including a vineyard. They had nine children and the youngest was my Tio Giuseppe, but they lovingly called him Peep for *Pepp-n-iell* because he was the runt of the family."

Jonah watched the sparkle in Lina's dark eyes, and the way her hands moved through the air when she talked. She almost crackled with energy—so different from Koko's stillness, her ability to blend into the earth.

"Every year, the family would make wine. They had a big wooden vat." She stretched her arms out. "About five or six feet high and six or seven feet wide. My grandfather, Nonno, in Italian, would make his own blend, using the grapes he grew as well as buying some from his neighbors. Nonno would go around the nearby farms sampling grapes, sometimes choosing them for their color, sometimes for their sweetness."

Jonah held up his glass, studying the rich burgundy color of the wine.

"Then, on a certain day, the farmers would deliver the grapes to the house. The men in the family would throw box after box of grape clusters into the vat. Next, they'd jump in barefooted, wearing old pants they'd cut short. Five or six men at once— brothers and brothers-in-law. They'd crush the grapes by stomping on them, until the men were splattered with purple from the chest down. People talked and joked and laughed as they worked."

Seeing the color of the wine in his glass, scenting the aroma, Jonah imagined the men making the wine he drank now.

Lina stopped to butter a roll and take a bite. Once she'd finished chewing, she resumed her story. "When Tio Peep was about five years old, he used a wooden crate to climb to the top of the vat and perch there, watching the men. He was so curious and wanted to stomp the grapes with the men, but he was too small. The sweet fumes rose into the air, making Peep lightheaded. Likewise, bees, big flies, and other insects buzzed around, then overcome by the fumes, and would fall into the vat."

Jonah eyed his wine in askance. *Insects?*

Nonna and my aunts were in the house cooking the meal. She came outside and hollered, '*Vieni a mangiare!* Come and eat.' The men climbed out and washed up at the pump. After they left, Peep tried to climb down, but he became unbalanced and fell into the vat, barely managing to grab the side. It was slicker than grease inside the barrel, and he couldn't climb out. He was breathing fumes, becoming weaker, and terrified he was going to drown." She gave a dramatic pause, then took some soup.

Jonah realized, in his fascination with her story, he'd stopped eating, and hurriedly spooned some minestrone into his mouth. "What happened then?"

"Nonna saw Peep's empty chair and asked where he was. The men said they'd left him sitting on the side of the vat. When they realized the danger, they ran outside. Peep was up to his neck in the mushy wine, barely hanging on. They grabbed him up, but he couldn't even talk because of the fumes. The men teased him about being drunk. I don't think he really was because the grapes hadn't been fermented. Then they stripped him and washed him under the pump. When Nonna found out, she gave her naked boy a big hug and cried because her baby almost drowned."

Jonah shook his head. "If that don't beat all," he drawled. He finished the last of his soup, then sat back in his chair, watching Lina's eyes sparkle with delight at her storytelling, and Adam eating his fill, and realized a long time had passed since he'd enjoyed an evening this much.

Chapter Fifteen

At the breakfast table two days later, Jonah announced he was going hunting for the third time in as many days.

"Again," Lina said in a sharp tone, setting her empty coffee cup on the table with a smack that made Adam's eyes widen. She reached over to pat the boy's shoulder, regretting her snappishness.

Her husband pushed away his empty plate and drank the last of his milk. "I'm going after turkeys today."

"That's three days in a row, Jonah. We have enough meat now. We need *everything* else!" Lina picked up the tin cup and waved it in the air. "This was the last of the coffee." She gestured toward the empty shelves of the kitchen. "There's almost nothing there! We *must* go to town today."

"A trip can wait."

She smacked the table with the palm of her hand. "*Non ci credo!*"

Adam's face puckered.

With difficulty, Lina reached deep inside for patience. "I can't believe this," she repeated more softly in English. "Jonah, I don't think you understand. I need to go to the store."

He raised his eyebrows. "How do you plan on getting there?"

"I'll give you a list, and you can go."

"Tomorrow," he evaded with a shake of his head. "I'm going hunting today."

"Jonah," she said with an edge in her voice. "I'd go myself but it's too far to walk and take Adam."

Jonah leaned forward. "You need to learn how to ride, Lina. I'll teach you." He raised his brows. "Or you can sit behind me on the horse. With Adam in front of me, though, I don't think we can bring much home."

Lina had a vision of herself, dress hiked above her knees, riding behind her husband, and she shuddered. "*Assolutamente no.*"

"English, Lina."

"Absolutely not," she said through clenched teeth.

"Then you'll have to wait 'til tomorrow."

"What about buying a wagon?"

He clenched his jaw and sat back in the chair. "Wagons don't grow on trees. It's a mighty big purchase. But I'll think on it."

Lina thought of the money she'd brought with her. Was it enough to buy a wagon? Did she want to use all her funds in that manner? *But this is important.* "I have some money you can use."

He frowned. "I don't want to take your money."

"It's *our* money, now."

"I'll think on it," he repeated and rose from the table.

How dare he leave without finishing the discussion? "Are you trying to keep me prisoner here?"

"Didn't I just offer to teach you to ride?" Jonah responded in a practical voice.

Frustration hit her. "*Madonna mia!*" Lina threw up her hands and stood with such fury that her chair almost fell over. She stormed into the bedroom, slamming the door behind her.

☙

Lina stood on the porch with the butter churn, which she'd found in the barn and cleaned in scalding water. Adam played a few feet away with the wooden wagon and tin soldiers. Today, he wasn't as clingy, although he needed her to stay in his sight or he became upset.

With Jonah gone for another day of hunting, and the bread and butter from Trudy's basket used up, Lina knew she could at least make butter, even if she didn't have the supplies to bake bread.

She'd poured the cream from the last two days into the wooden churn and began to pump the churn-dash up and down, up and down, using the motion to release some of the anger and panic that had been bubbling inside ever since the argument with her husband.

Without transportation, she was trapped on the farm, and the thought frightened her. She knew marriage, especially a mail-order marriage, meant giving a man power over her, but she hadn't thought through all of what that could mean. If Jonah refused to buy a wagon or a buggy, then she couldn't attend church, or go to town when she needed supplies, or send and receive mail, or visit Trudy... With each tick of the list, her stomach tightened. *I'll have to learn to ride.* But the idea was overwhelming.

The butter started to form, and the up-and-down motion of the churn-dash became more difficult. Her breathing grew jagged, and her arms ached. She stopped to catch her breath and rest her arms before beginning again.

No wonder Aunt Sophia has always been so strong.

The sound of hoofbeats and the jingle of a harness made Lina look up to see Trudy driving a wagon into the yard. Excitement, relief, and love flooded her heart. *When did she learn to drive?*

Lina let out a glad gasp, wiped her sleeve across her damp face, and rubbed her hands on her apron.

Trudy set the brake and swung down from the wagon seat. She carried a crocheted reticule and wore a nice blue shirtwaist and skirt.

Like a girl, Lina raced across the hard-packed dirt to throw herself at her friend. "Trudy, Trudy!" She gave her a big hug, inhaling the scent of lavender. "It's so good to see you!"

"Land sakes, Lina. You just saw me four days ago." Trudy straightened her arms and studied Lina's face. "What's wrong? Is it Adam? Jonah? He's not mistreating you, is he?"

"No. No... Oh, Trudy," Lina almost wailed. "This life here is not what I expected."

Adam started to cry.

Trudy tugged Lina toward the porch. "Good thing I came today. Come and tell me everything."

Lina hurried over to scoop up Adam, who stopped crying. Holding him, she took a seat on the bench.

Trudy perched next to her. "You need a rocking chair, Lina."

"I need a lot more than a rocking chair." She kissed Adam and set him on his feet, then sent an embarrassed look to her friend. "I can't even offer you tea or coffee. We're out."

Adam toddled back to his toys and plopped down next to the wagon.

Once Lina saw him pick up a soldier, she turned to Trudy. "Before I start, tell me when you learned to drive the wagon. I couldn't believe my eyes when I saw you holding the reins."

Trudy laughed. "Seth has let me practice to and from town. But today was the first time I've driven on my own. He made me recite the way to your farm five times before he let me go. And I have strict orders to be home before dark."

Lina shook her head in admiration. "Who would have thought...?"

Trudy raised one eyebrow. "Frontier living is definitely a challenge. I predict we both will learn far more than we ever dreamed back in St. Louis."

Lina sighed. "If only we had a wagon for me to learn to drive. Or even a cart. Driving horses don't seem as frightening as riding them." She leaned her head back against the wall of the house. "The worst is the isolation." Lina stopped. "Well, actually it's not quite that. It's the fact that I can't go to town if I want to. We desperately need supplies, but Jonah insists on hunting to replenish the larder, instead of going to the store. Our icebox is full and the rest of the game is in the icehouse. He brought back a deer the first day. About scared the living daylights out of me when I saw him carrying the bloody carcass over his shoulders."

"I would imagine so," Trudy murmured.

"The next day, squirrels, and then yesterday, it was rabbits."

"Goodness me! I know Seth hunts, but he's been too busy." She shook her head. "I'm sure cooking game is in my future."

Lina grimaced. "While game is well and good, I can't make bread with it or desserts. I'm just glad I brought so much with me. And I'm also grateful you left us the basket. We ate the last of your bread and butter yesterday. *Butter*." Lina jumped to her feet and hurried to the churn. "Just let me finish this up." She lifted the churn cover to peer inside. The sour smell of buttermilk greeted her.

Trudy rose and came over. "Looks like you're about ready."

"This is the first time I've made my own butter."

"Well, you've done a good job. You need to pour off the buttermilk and thoroughly rinse the lump in cold water. Do you know how to make buttermilk pancakes and biscuits?"

Lina flashed Trudy a smile, feeling better already. "Dona showed us at the agency. Bertha, of course, made the best pancakes of all of us."

"Of course!" Trudy echoed. "I envy Bertha's baking, that I do."

"And her biscuits! I brought some fresh baked ones home to Nonna. When she tasted them, my grandmother was almost ready to marry off Bertha to one of my cousins. If Bertha had been Italian, Nonna probably would have shown up at the agency and carried her away.

Trudy laughed. "I can just see that happening." She looked down at the butter. "Do you have a wooden paddle?"

"Yes, let me go get it."

"Scald the paddle first. We'll cool it under the pump water."

Grateful for the directions, Lina hastened into the house for the paddle.

The two women continued the chore of butter making, until a block of butter wrapped in waxed paper rested on a shelf in the icebox. Lina gave the butter a look of satisfaction before she closed the door and turned to her friend.

Trudy waved toward the direction of the wagon. "Come help me unload."

"Unload?"

"I brought you a side table you can place between the chairs. And another lamp—I seem to have a dozen of them." Her hand waved in the air. "Then, when I was at the mercantile, I asked the Cobbs—they're the owners—if they'd met you. When they said they hadn't, I became worried, knowing the empty state of your pantry. So I filled the grocery order with what I imagined you'd want. Then I stopped by Mrs. Murphy's and bought some of her pullets. Luckily, she likes me, so she didn't charge an arm and a leg for the chickens like she probably would you."

"Oh, *Trudy*. Thank you. And I certainly hope you kept careful accounting so I can pay you back."

"Here." Trudy fished a piece of paper out of her reticule and handed it over. "Oh, I almost forgot. I went to get the mail and told Mr. Waite I was heading here. He gave me a letter for you. It's from Heather, and I'm dying to know what she's written."

Lina scanned the receipt and let out a relieved breath when she saw the amount. She had more than enough money to cover Trudy's expenditures. "Let me get this for you right away. Then we'll unload, and I'll see how well you've judged the needs of an Italian cook." She sent Trudy a teasing smile. "After that, we'll read Heather's letter."

They took everything out of the wagon and into the house. With fresh cups of coffee from the replenished supply, they sat on the porch bench, watching the five black pullets Trudy had brought make themselves at home by scratching in the dirt of the yard.

Adam was fascinated by the chickens and crouched several feet away from them. From the intense expression on her son's face, Lina figured that soon he would stop studying the pullets and start chasing them.

Lina opened the letter and began to read aloud.

Dearest Lina,

I am so sorry I caused you such distress with my letter. I did not know who else to turn to when my whole world fell apart around my feet. Now that I am settled at the boardinghouse in town, I can take my time and tell you the whole, unbelievable story.

First, Hayden did not write the letter to Mrs. Seymour, as we thought. It was written by his mother, Ina, who, after I forgave her for her meddling ways, has become very dear to me. She is a most sweet woman and only wanted her son to settle down and find a nice wife like Evie, whom she has become quite attached to.

Yes, you are correct in what you are thinking, Hayden did not even know I existed until the day I showed up at his house ready to become his wife! He was shocked, and understandably so, as any man would be.

With a gasp, Lina dropped the letter and exchanged appalled glances with Trudy. *What a cruel trick to play on Heather.*

Trudy was the first to speak. "I can't believe his mother wrote for a bride!"

Lina thought back to a conversation she'd had with Heather. "We knew there was something odd about that letter, but Mrs. Seymour spoke so highly of the family. Her testimony was what persuaded Heather to accept the match."

Trudy shook her head. "Oh, dear Lord. Poor Heather." She waved to the letter. "What else does she say?"

Lina resumed.

But even then, Hayden was kind to me and did not take his annoyance over the situation out on his mother. He has been a true gentleman in all ways. However, he has not changed his mind about marrying me, or anyone. He says he is a confirmed bachelor. So, as you now understand, I do not have any wedding details to share. That will make receiving yours that much more delightful.

"Oh!" Lina smacked the letter against her leg. She jumped up and paced across the porch, brandishing the paper. "That man is refusing to do right by Heather. Why I...I..." Words failed her...or at least English words failed her, and Trudy wouldn't understand the torrent of Italian she wanted to unleash. With effort, Lina held back a flood of recriminations.

Trudy laughed, then pulled a face. "I'm not amused by

Heather's situation, but by the thought of you giving Mr. Klinkner a piece of your mind. The man's lucky you aren't in Y Knot. He's lucky we *both* aren't. I don't think he'd withstand two angry Mail-Order Brides of the West. And I'm sure Evie would join us, and that would make *three* angry brides against him."

"Three angry brides and my wooden spoon!" Lina let out a breath and sat on the bench. "I wonder why Heather isn't staying with Evie?" She smoothed out the letter and began to read.

Even though Hayden will not be my husband, I will describe him so you can better understand my letters when you receive them. He is tall, same height as Morgan—Oh, thank you for sending me my brother! It was with joy that I heard his voice at the boardinghouse, even before I saw his face. What a welcome surprise! With Morgan by my side, I am much more able to hold my head up in this town where everyone knows my embarrassing plight.

But I digress. Now back to Hayden. He is incredibly handsome. He has sandy colored blond hair, with soft baby-like curls, not quite as curly as yours. When it is wet, it shrinks up much shorter than normal. I know this because one day while I was still living at the Klinkner's, he went for a swim in the river and I caught him as he climbed out of the chilly water. We were both quite embarrassed, but still, I was glad it happened.

His eyes are a vivid blue that seem to hold secrets of his own. Mostly, he is happy, has a good sense of humor, and likes to tease me. Now that I have moved, I will miss our morning conversations over breakfast and coffee.

Troubled, Lina lowered her hand to her lap. She bit her lip and stared at Trudy. "Heather loves him."

Trudy set a hand to her chest. "My heart breaks for her. Heather is such a lovely woman and a hard worker." She inhaled a deep breath. "If Hayden Klinkner doesn't come around soon, we'll have to invite her to Sweetwater Springs. Why, I've met a dozen bachelors I could introduce her to." She clasped her hands together. "Some worthy man will snap her up in an instant. How lovely having Heather with us would be."

Lina sighed. "A change of town probably won't do any good. Not if she loves him." She picked up the letter and continued reading.

The day after I arrived the steam engine blew, breaking Hayden's father's leg—the poor man—he had a very bad go of it. But he is doing much better. The next day, I made the chicken recipe you showed us girls! I was so proud of myself. Remember the one in the clay pot? Ina had a good selection of spices, and although I could not remember exactly everything you said to do, I improvised a little. It turned out delicious, and everyone was delighted and thought it the best chicken they had ever had. Thank you, dear friend!

You are so blessed that you will be living in Sweetwater Springs with Trudy. How I miss her! Tell her I will be writing to her soon.

Trudy's hand fluttered. "I'll write to her right away. Do you think she'll mind that you shared her letter?"

Lina pursed her lips, thought about Heather's reaction, and then shook her head. "No. You two are friends. I'm sure she'll need all the support we can give her."

"Does Heather say anything about Evie?"

"Let's see." Lina glanced at the letter and silently skimmed ahead, then backtracked and read aloud.

I have seen Evie twice! She looks beautiful, and Chance is as handsome as Mrs. Seymour said. I visited her house tonight—built by Chance for her. Small, with one bedroom, but the inside is as charming as can be, and the grandfather clock from the agency, is a lovely addition to her home. Unfortunately for me, it was dark when I arrived, so I was unable to see any of the gorgeous views that I have been hearing about and longing to see. If her surroundings are anything like the rest of Montana that I have seen, she is a very lucky girl to live in such beauty.

Please forgive me for such a long letter, but writing it makes me feel as if you are here. I would tell you more about Hayden, but I truly do not know more myself.

I want to hear more of your Jonah Barrett! All I know is what everyone learned that morning around the breakfast table when you announced—to my utter surprise—your acceptance of his proposal, and that was not much at all. How old is he? What does he look like? You said he had an Indian wife before—does he speak her language? Perhaps you can teach him Italian and he can teach you Blackfoot. It sounds exciting—and to be truthful, a little daunting to me. But, if anyone can do it, it is you, my friend. You must not second-guess yourself. He will love you! How could he not! With your past position as governess, you have all the qualifications to make his little son a wonderful mother. In no time at all, you will be a happy family.

So, as always, I am sending you all my love. We must stay strong and positive. As soon as I know more of my situation here, I will write again. Also, I will be dutiful in checking at Lichtenstein's store—how could I not since I now work there—for another of your letters.

Be happy, my dear friend!

~Heather

Lina's voice trailed off, and she had to sniff back sudden tears. Trudy rested her hand on Lina's arm.

"We had such high hopes when we received our matches," Lina said, her voice thick. "We were so confident because we had personal recommendations about Hayden and Jonah. And now both Heather and I are unhappy…" her voice trailed off.

Trudy squeezed Lina's arm. "You've only had four days to adjust to each other. Jonah's a good man, Lina. He's rough around the edges and will need…*sanding.*" Her tone brightened at the metaphor. "He's had such a different life. Give him time to adjust to you, to the idea of being part of a community."

Puzzled, Lina glanced at Trudy. "What do you mean?"

"From what Seth has told me, Jonah's lived a very isolated life. And marrying an Indian woman did not help matters. When I was at the mercantile inquiring about you…" She made a face and looked out over the field. "Mrs. Cobb had a very condemning attitude toward him—not in what she said, but in her expressions. But Mrs. Cobb is quite a shewish character, and I'd dismiss any judgment of hers. But other people were in the store, and they, too, exchanged censorious looks." She shrugged helplessly. "You know the type." She laid a gentle hand on Lina's arm. "And has anyone been to call on you?"

Lina shook her head. "I didn't even think about that. I've been so busy…so far away from anyone." Her stomach felt heavy as if she'd swallowed a stone.

"You're just what Jonah needs to restore his reputation. Once he partakes in the social activities of the town, things will change.

You'll see." Trudy's tone sounded confident. "We must do what we can to restore his reputation and involve him in community life. A wife will help." She gave Lina an impish smile. "Having one certainly has for Seth."

Lina wasn't so sure. More than ever, she wondered if she'd jumped into a far deeper pond than she'd expected. The water was over her head, and she wasn't the best swimmer.

"I'll introduce you to the town leaders with whom I'm acquainted. They are kind people—at least, the ones I've met."

"If I never go to town, you won't have a chance to make introductions. I might never see any of these people."

"Nonsense," Trudy said in a brisk tone. "It's not like you to be so pessimistic. You must cultivate a cheerful attitude and believe all will turn out for the best."

She's right. I have been allowing my fears to take over.

"I think I have a partial solution. I met the Dunns at church. They own the ranch between here and town. On our way home after your wedding, Seth pointed out the road to their house." She turned to Lina, her eyes sparkling. "Why don't we go call on them? I'll bet they'll even insist on giving you a ride home."

A visit! Lina jumped to her feet. "That would be lovely!" She glanced down at her housedress. "Let me put on a nicer dress and clean up Adam."

"While you're changing, I'll write a note for Jonah. Do you have paper?"

"Yes, in my trunk. Be sure and tell him to heat up the soup if I'm not back in time for supper."

Lina made short work of washing Adam and changing him out of his Indian chamois clothing, giving herself a sponge bath, donning her second-best dress, and tidying her hair. Not long had passed before she returned to the main room, Adam in her arms. She set him down and checked the stove, noting that the fire had died down to coals. She moved the pot to the very back of the stove where it could keep for the few hours she'd be away. Then she took her hat and red shawl from off the antler rack.

Lina turned to Trudy. "Now for the first step in our plan."

Chapter Sixteen

Carrying two turkeys, their feet tied together and slung over his shoulders, Jonah trudged toward home. After four straight days of hunting, providing venison, squirrels, rabbit, and now turkey, he considered he'd done a right fair job of stocking up the larder. Surely now, Lina would see that they could live off the land with only a few trips to town.

Although he hadn't liked Lina being angry this morning, he'd carried the memory of her with him—the way her dark eyes snapped and the color blazed in her cheeks, the animation of her moving hands. He'd felt guilty for riling her up and resolved to make it up to her. *I'll go to town tomorrow.* Even the thought of a dreaded trip to Sweetwater Springs wasn't enough to dim his excitement at seeing his wife when he returned home.

When he reached the house, neither his wife nor his son was in sight. Jonah dropped the turkey carcasses on the porch bench and hurried inside, feeling a sting of alarm. The silence caught him by surprise. Since Koko's death, he'd lived with the emptiness of his home. In the brief time Lina had lived here, she'd filled the place with warmth, with humming and words, and with enticing smells. The more he'd gotten to know her, the more he enjoyed the changes she'd made in his life and the more attracted to her he'd become.

Without her, the space echoed with silence. He knew without even calling her name that his wife and son weren't in the house. But just in case, he headed for the bedroom. Lina had told him she'd taken naps with Adam.

When he saw the empty bed, he whirled and ran outside. "Lina!" Jonah called. "Adam!" He shaded his eyes against the sun to check if they were in the garden, but he saw no sight of them.

Koko's horse grazed in the pasture, but he doubted Lina would have ridden. *How the heck did they leave?*

Loping past the garden she'd planted yesterday and toward the barn, he yelled. "Lina!" But received no answer. Blood pounded in his ears. *Where are they?*

Inside the barn, the cow gave him a curious stare, but his wife and son weren't there, either.

She's left me and taken Adam! Jonah's stomach cramped. Fear swamped his brain. All he could think of was that he should have found a way to get her to town like she'd wanted. Instead, he'd left his bride—a stranger to Sweetwater Springs, to this country life—all alone for days. No wonder she'd left him. And since she'd taken Adam, she must not think he was a good father. Pain radiated through him.

Jonah trudged back to the house, his steps heavy. Once inside, the first thing that caught his attention was the red-and-white tablecloth. *She didn't take it with her!* With a spurt of hope he glanced around and spotted the minestrone pot on the stove, then a marble-topped table placed between the two leather chairs. *Where did that come from?*

Hurrying to the bedroom, Jonah saw Lina's trunk in the corner. With a deep breath of gladness, he realized that she hadn't left him. *Then where in tarnation are they?*

Feeling foolish for his reaction, he returned to the main room and noticed the sheet of paper resting on the colorful tablecloth. With two long strides, he reached the table, snatched up the note, and read. When Jonah finished, his shoulders relaxed, although it took a lot longer for his heartbeat to slow. Holding the letter in his hands, he realized he stood at a crossroads in his marriage. *Home and safety.* He glanced around. *Emptiness.*

Jonah looked down at his bloodstained buckskins and bit off a curse. Seeing him like this would probably scare off Lina.

Slowly, Jonah walked outside and sank down on the porch step. He could hardly haul Lina and Adam back home. Calling on the neighbors was a perfectly natural occurrence, even if, for his part, no visiting had taken place between the Barretts and the Dunns for twenty years.

Buried memories resurfaced. He recalled his ma being right friendly with Mrs. Dunn. The Dunns had tried to call several times after Ma's death, and, as with Reverend Norton, his pa had run them off with drunken shouts and some wild pot shots with his rifle.

Mrs. Dunn had even braved Hardy's saloon a time or two to beg his father to allow Jonah to come stay with them for a few days. All she'd received in return for her kindness were growls and insults. Later, she'd tried to talk to Jonah alone, but his pain and shame had rendered him practically mute.

That shame rose again. He could have visited the Dunns any time in the years since his pa's death. *No, I should have visited once I became a man and Pa had no say over me.*

So, why didn't I?

That required more contemplation. His thoughts in the past, Jonah watched some young chickens peck at the dirt near the far corner of the porch. Minutes passed before he realized the birds were real and not his mother's chickens. Trudy must have brought them for Lina.

Knowing that a friend had done for his wife what he should have made shame tighten his stomach. *Why did I isolate myself? Why did I allow this situation to come to pass?*

Jonah hadn't always avoided Sweetwater Springs. As a boy, he had loved going to church and school. He'd plenty of friends and the townsfolk respected his parents.

Jonah forced himself to remember the years he tried to forget—when his father became the town drunkard—the man who'd drink until he collapsed into a heap, muttering and stinking of whisky. His condition wasn't so bad at the saloon. Hardy would drag Sam Barrett to an out-of-the-way corner and let him sleep it off. Jonah would play with Seth, who was the son of a saloon girl. She saw to it that he was fed, and if necessary, he slept with Seth on his friend's pallet on the floor.

No, it was his father's public behavior, when he lay in a drunken stupor in the street for all to see, which had marked Jonah, made him a lone wolf. For many years, Jonah wasn't strong enough to move Pa's heavy body. The disapproving glances directed at his pa cut him to the quick. When he grew older, Jonah saw those same looks directed at him whenever he went into the saloon, and later, when he married a squaw.

What made me refuse to go to town when Lina asked?

Jonah took a deep breath, facing the truth.

He'd been a coward. In hiding, Jonah had caused strife in his new marriage. *Have I damaged my relationship with Lina beyond repair?*

Resolutely, Jonah reached for the dressed, trussed-up birds and unworked the rope from around the feet of the plumpest. He'd take the big tom turkey as a gift to the Dunns. He was not about to show up empty-handed. *I have years of unfriendliness to atone for.*

❦

Trudy drew up the horses in front of a long, narrow ranch house with a wide, welcoming porch, and tied off the reins. "This is a beautiful place," she said with a trace of envy in her tone. "Bigger than ours."

Away from the tall trees of the forest, it was easier to see the mountains. The foothills of the nearest one sloped down to the outskirts of the lush grazing land. A warm breeze blew across the meadow that stretched to the left of the house. In the middle, a solitary oak spread sheltering branches over a wooden table flanked by benches. A small stream meandered through the grass. On the other side of the house, a big red barn rose above outbuildings and a fenced garden and small orchard.

The ranch looked far more prosperous than Jonah's farm and, with sudden nervousness, Lina wondered what the Dunns would think of her, especially since she was a mail-order bride. *Will they judge me? Turn us away?*

A woman wearing a brown riding habit and a man's leather hat strode out of the barn toward the house. A black-and-white dog trotted at her side. She saw the wagon, checked her stride, and changed direction toward the guests.

The dog raced ahead of her barking.

Drawing closer, the woman obviously recognized Trudy and gave the two of them a wide smile. "Hush, Patches. They're friends."

The dog ceased barking and wagged its tail.

The woman stopped at the side of the wagon. "Mrs. Flanigan. A bit out of the way aren't you?" Her gaze flicked to Lina and back to Trudy.

"Most definitely, Mrs. Dunn. However, I wanted to presume on our brief acquaintanceship and introduce you to my friend, Lina Napolitano." She placed a hand on Lina's shoulder. "Well, she's married to Jonah Barrett now, so she's no longer Miss Napolitano."

"Delighted to meet you, Mrs. Barrett. I had no idea Jonah married again." Mrs. Dunn gave Adam a curious glance. "Although with a little one, that's all to the best." She gave Lina a direct look. "Are you a mail-order bride too?"

Mrs. Dunn's matter of fact question eased some of Lina's nervousness. "Yes, ma'am. We're both from St. Louis."

Mrs. Dunn waved her hand in a dismissive gesture. "Call me Addie. No need to be formal between neighbors." She gestured to the house. "Please come in and sit a while. Not often do we have visitors. I'll have someone see to your horses." She turned, shouted to a man grooming a horse outside the barn, and motioned him over.

"Let me come around, Mrs. Barrett, and take that sweet boy

from you while you climb down. Except for his coloring, he looks just like his father at the same age. Many a time I held young Jonah."

"Please, Addie, if we're to be on a first-name basis, I'm Lina."

"Trudy," her friend chimed in.

"All right." Addie flashed a wide smile, walked around the back of the wagon, and reached up for Adam.

With some uncertainty, Lina handed him over, and when Addie stepped back, she hurried to climb down lest Adam set up a squawk.

The child watched to make sure she was next to him, but he allowed Addie to hold him—until Trudy joined them, and then he reached for Lina.

"Progress," Lina said, taking back her son. "He cried the first time Trudy held him, and we haven't tried since."

Addie waved toward the house. "Please, step inside and sit a while." She led them to the porch.

The door opened, and a plump woman with wooly gray-streaked blond hair and a square chin stuck her head out. Her pale blue eyes had a curious gleam. "I thought I heard the sound of a wagon."

"Ladies, Mrs. Pendell is our cook and housekeeper. I don't know what I'd do without her."

"Cook a lot more meals," Mrs. Pendell retorted with a teasing smile.

"Mrs. P, these ladies are Sweetwater Springs' Mail-Order Brides. Mrs. Seth Flanigan and Mrs. Jonah Barrett."

At the mention of their married names, Trudy and Lina exchanged pleased smiles.

Addie laughed. "The newness hasn't worn off, has it?"

"It's my first time being introduced as Mrs. Jonah Barrett," Lina explained.

Mrs. Pendell clapped her hands. "A celebration is in store." She ushered them inside and gestured to a doorway. "Have a seat, and I'll be right in with refreshments. Too bad I haven't baked a cake. But I've got cookies cooling, and you're lucky the hands haven't been in to snatch 'em up yet."

"Sounds lovely." Lina relaxed at the warmth and welcome from the two women.

"Would you like coffee or tea?" Mrs. Pendell asked.

After the three of them chose tea, Addie gave Mrs. Pendell her Stetson and led them into a spacious parlor with leather chairs, a settee upholstered in worn gold velvet, and a stove near the back.

Lina and Trudy chose the settee, and Addie took a seat in a chair across from them. Lina placed Adam on the floor, smoothing his hair.

He stood and watched Addie with a grave expression, his hand resting on Lina's knee.

Addie studied them with calm gray eyes. She had a plain face and wore her thick brown hair in a braid down her back. "I haven't spoken to Jonah in years, although not for want of trying. His mother and I were dear friends, and he was the sweetest boy."

Lina glanced down at Adam, who stared at Mrs. Dunn with wide eyes, and could imagine the innocent little child Jonah must have been.

"Our families were quite close until Patience and the baby died, and everything changed."

"Patience?" A name Lina didn't recognize.

"Jonah's mother. She died in childbirth and her second son with her."

Lina sucked in a shocked breath. "His mother and brother *and* his wife and daughter died in childbirth?" *Poor, poor Jonah!*

"And his grandmother, although her babe lived."

Madonna Mia. Lina crossed herself. "So heartbreaking." Her family had never lost a mother to childbirth, although one of her aunts and a cousin had given birth to stillborn babies, tragedies both times.

Trudy frowned, her hands clasped tightly in her lap. "Is it common that so many mothers and babies die out here."

"For many years, we didn't have a doctor," Addie said simply.

"Ah," Lina said in relief. "Mrs. Norton assures us that Dr. Cameron is quite competent."

"Absolutely. The doctor didn't attend to Jonah's wife. Perhaps if he had…" Addie brushed her hands together. "Well, the tragedy has led you to Sweetwater Springs, Lina. St. Louis, eh," she said, obviously changing the subject. "I'm from Philadelphia, myself."

Trudy raised her eyebrows. "However, did you end up in Montana?"

Addie grinned. "You wouldn't believe it to look at me…I was a sickly girl, and on the advice of our doctor, my parents sent me to the country in hopes that being out in nature would strengthen me. I wasn't headed for Montana, but I met my husband on the train. During the trip, he convinced me to get off at Sweetwater Springs and marry him."

Trudy brought a hand to her chest. "So romantic."

"The stories I could tell you. I was a pampered young lady." Addie waved her hand toward the window. "As green as that grass out there. I didn't even know how to cook. Not that I had to that often, thank goodness. Harrison, my husband, already had Mrs. Pendell, and she taught me to whip up a tolerable meal. More importantly, I can garden, ride a horse in all terrains, rope a steer, kill a chicken, shoot a varmint…all *ladylike*—" she said the word in a droll manner "—*accomplishments* I learned after living here for a while."

Well, at least I can cook and garden, Lina tried to reassure herself. "You were brave taking such a risk."

Addie raised one eyebrow. "I'm talking to two mail-order brides, and you call *me* brave."

The three of them burst out laughing.

Lina reached over and patted her friend's knee. "Trudy is the bravest because she came here first—to an unknown town to wed a stranger. She wrote to me about Sweetwater Springs and about my husband. With a friend's favorable recommendation my choice wasn't as frightening as hers was."

"I'm sure you both will thrive here." Addie waved a hand down her body. "As you see, I'm as healthy as a horse. A Montana marriage *with the right man* is good for body and soul." Her expression sobered. "As I hope you both will experience for yourselves. But…your men don't have the best reputations, although neither is considered a bad man."

Trudy and Lina glanced at each other.

Lina took a deep breath. "That's partly why we came here. I would like us—my husband and myself—to have more involvement in the town." She frowned. "One of my stumbling blocks is that I don't know how to ride a horse."

Addie leaned forward, obviously about to say something.

Lina held up a hand to forestall her. "I'm not saying I won't learn eventually. However, I know nothing about horses, and the very idea frightens me. Right now, I need to focus on Adam." She patted the boy's shoulder. "He's clinging to me and won't let me leave his sight. I need to organize the household and plant the garden…" She shook her head, and her shoulders drooped. "So much to do. It's overwhelming, really."

Addie gave a slow nod of understanding. "And Jonah doesn't have a wagon, so you can't drive to town."

"Precisely," Trudy said.

Addie sat back in her chair. "On Sunday, we could certainly pick you up and take you to church. If you cut through the woods, the walk between your farm and our road to town is not far. A path used to run through there. No doubt it's overgrown, but you still should be able to pass along it."

Even though Addie's suggestion was what Lina wanted, the offer was still hard to accept, for it meant missing the Catholic prayer meeting she'd looked forward to. But she couldn't ask the Dunns to wait around town after the Protestant service was over. Hopefully, this arrangement would just be temporary. *Surely we'll purchase a wagon soon.*

But what if Jonah refuses?

Chapter Seventeen

Jonah rode his gelding Scout up to the Dunn ranch and reined in, surveying his surroundings. The long, low house looked smaller than he remembered but still far more substantial than his own. Of course, the Dunns were one of the earliest families to settle in Sweetwater Springs, long before his parents arrived as a young couple from the east.

The house had three bedrooms, he remembered, and a parlor that was separated from the kitchen. To a young boy, that much space had seemed immense. Jonah recalled playing with Tyler Dunn, who'd been only a little older than Adam's age at the time. He'd envied the boy having his own bedroom.

A big red barn had replaced a far smaller structure. He recognized Seth's unhitched wagon by the wall. The ladies weren't sitting in the rocking chairs on the porch. Maybe they were inside eating cookies in Mrs. Pendell's kitchen.

Harrison Dunn walked out of the barn, carrying a pitchfork. He saw Jonah, leaned the tool against the wall, and ambled over. He tipped back the brim of his hat and smiled. "Well, look who's here. I often wondered if I'd see the day when you'd come riding up, Jonah Barrett. Addie is going to be over the moon to see you."

Jonah's return smile felt creaky, his facial muscles stiff. "Good to see you, too." He gestured to the wagon. "My bride and Seth Flanigan's wife have come to visit."

Mr. Dunn grabbed his hat and smacked it against his leg. "If that don't beat all! I've been out riding, just got back. You have a new wife? And she's here with Flanigan's mail-order bride? That man sure got lucky. Darn pretty filly."

"Yep." Jonah swung down from Scout. "You have *two* mail-order brides and a little boy around here somewhere." After unhooking the turkey from the saddle horn, he held out the bird. "I had good hunting today. Got plenty. Thought you'd like one."

Mr. Dunn took the turkey from him and hefted up the bird to admire it. "Been a while since we had us a turkey dinner. Mrs. P will be right pleased with this. Thank you, son."

Son. The affection behind the word made his throat tighten. Until this minute, Jonah hadn't realized his relationship with the Dunns was another thing he'd lost when his mother died. The couple had always been warm and welcoming, like extended family. Once again he regretted not renewing the friendship long ago.

Mr. Dunn made a *come on* gesture. "Let's go find our wives, shall we?" He signaled to one of the hands who'd been watching from the open barn door, and the man came trotting over. "See to the horse, will ya, Blake?"

The man gave a nod and took the reins from Jonah, leading Scout to the barn.

They walked up to the porch and entered the house. Mr. Dunn paused, but the sound of feminine laughter made him turn right to the parlor instead of left into the kitchen.

Jonah followed.

The conversation ceased when they entered the room. Lina saw him and let out a gasp, her eyes widening, and a slow smile spreading over her face.

"Paa." Adam smiled at him.

"Oh, my!" Addie set down her cup, flew at Jonah, and gave him a fierce hug. She stepped back and studied his face, her eyes bright. "My dear boy, how good it is to see you."

"And you too, ma'am." Jonah dipped his chin in acknowledgement.

"I've been speaking with your delightful wife and her friend, Trudy. How smart of you, dear boy, to send for a bride. Just what this town needs. Fresh blood of the feminine variety."

Her welcome made a ball of warmth blaze in Jonah's belly. Yet, he couldn't help feeling guilty about not having visited earlier. "I'm sorry, I haven't been a good neighbor...a good friend."

Addie's expression softened. "We understood. You're here now, and that's what matters. Sit down, dear." She waved Jonah to a leather chair, then looked over at her husband. "Harrison, will you have Mrs. Pendell bring you and Jonah some tea?"

When Mr. Dunn returned, he was carrying two plates, with teacups on saucers placed on top. Napkins draped over one of his arms. He gave one stack and a napkin to Jonah.

Addie handed Jonah the cookie plate.

He took one, feeling awkward.

"Tyler is out checking on the herd," Addie told him. "Hopefully, he'll make it back before you leave."

Jonah thought of the little boy he'd played with and felt old. "I've glimpsed him around town a time or too. Hard to believe he's grown into a man."

Addie beamed. "I know we shouldn't be boasting, but he's our only chick, and we are proud of him. He's grown into as fine a rancher as his father."

"I just wish he had his father's good instincts with women." Harrison growled with a shake of his head.

Jonah wondered if there was gossip of Tyler womanizing or keeping low company. He knew so little of town life or of his neighbors.

Addie reached for a cookie and set it on her plate. "Tyler's started courting a girl in town. We're not very fond of her and have tried to dissuade him. But he's set his sights on this young woman and is very determined." She sent her husband a fond smile. "He's like his father that way."

Harrison crossed his arms. "More like she set her sights on him."

Addie shrugged. "But what can you do?"

"Maybe when you become better acquainted with her—" Lina offered "—you'll find you like her after all."

Addie sighed. "We can only pray."

The conversation changed to talk of ranching matters. Soon after, the sound of boot heels on the wooden hallway floor heralded Tyler Dunn's entrance. He stood in the doorway and surveyed the company, giving the two brides a nod and polite smile, which widened when he saw Jonah. Crossing the room, he extended his hand, saying, "Well, I'll be" to convey his happiness at seeing his old playmate.

Tyler stood somewhat shorter than Jonah and had his father's rugged features and his mother's gray eyes. When he noticed Adam standing at Lina's knee, he stepped over to the boy and crouched down in front of him. "Hello, little fella."

"Ba."

Tyler laughed. "Ba, yourself." He ruffled Adam's hair, then stood. "I'll be right back."

Addie's eyes were alight with laughter. "When Tyler was Adam's age, *Ba* was his favorite word. Harrison took to calling him Little Sheep."

Mr. Dunn pretended to frown. "Hard for a cattle rancher to hear his son making sheep noises."

Tyler came back into the room, carrying something in his hand. Once again, he crouched in front of Adam and uncurled his fingers, exposing a carved wooden animal.

Adam studied the toy with serious eyes. Undecided, he looked up at Tyler.

"Go ahead, take it. It's a sheep. Can you say sheep? *Ba*."

"Ba," Adam mimicked.

The adults laughed.

Emboldened by their reaction, Adam grinned, reached for the animal, and picked the toy up. Obviously entranced, he plopped on his bottom to examine his treasure.

Jonah let out a long breath he hadn't known he was holding. The acceptance of the Dunns, the warmth in the room, soothed a hurt inside him that had ached for a long time. He glanced at Lina and saw understanding in her eyes. Something stretched between them, an acknowledgment of their union and a connection, as tenuous and delicate as a spider web, just as beautiful...*and dangerous.*

༄

The next evening, Lina finished setting the table and stepped out on the porch to ring the bell that hung on the corner of the roof to summon Jonah to supper. As usual, he seemed to sense when the meal was ready, and she saw him washing up at the pump barrel in the yard. He'd taken off his shirt and stood with his back to her, splashing his torso. For a minute, she watched the muscles of his back move and wondered what running her hands over them would be like, feeling his skin under her palms. Lina caught her amorous thoughts and, with heated cheeks, turned to go inside.

A movement from the corner of her eye made her pause and look down the road. Squinting, she made out a man leading what looked like a loaded pack mule. "Jonah," she called. "We have company."

He glanced over to the path, grabbed a towel, and dried off.

From the leisurely way he donned his shirt, Lina figured he was acquainted with the man.

Buttoning his shirt, he walked over to Lina. "Our nearest neighbor to the south. Gideon Walker."

"Ah, the hermit who made the wardrobe."

"Yes. He's an odd man. Shy. Intellectual. He's read every one of my books—twice."

"Well, he's come at the right time. Invite him to join us for supper."

"Lina," Jonah said in an urgent tone, his brow furrowed. "I

don't think Gid knows about Koko's death. I haven't seen him for months, and he may not have been to town."

"I'll go into the house then, to let you explain. But I'll set another place at the table."

He grabbed her hand and squeezed. "Thank you for understanding."

Feeling tingles from Jonah's touch and happy about his appreciation, Lina drifted into the house and surveyed the table, imagining the setting through a stranger's eyes. She wished she had nicer dishes but figured a hermit probably wouldn't care. Earlier, she'd added fresh flowers to the Mason jar on Trudy's doily, which made the table fancy enough for company.

Lina glanced at Adam playing on the floor with his sheep, soldiers, and wagon, and then hurried to grab a plate and dish up the food. She didn't imagine her husband and the shy Mr. Walker would have too many words between them, even about such momentous topics as the death of one wife and the acquisition of another. She doubted the food would have a chance to get cold.

With the supplies Trudy delivered, Lina had added potatoes and carrots to the venison minestrone and had baked bread. She hadn't intended to bring out a jar of jam but this was a special occasion. She set the huckleberry on the table, since they'd used up the strawberry jam. On the other side of the Mason jar, she put a crusty loaf of brown bread and a small bowl of her butter.

Lina was proven right about the length of male conversation.

Less than ten minutes later, Jonah stuck his head in the door and asked her to come outside. The two men stood on the porch, a small chest of drawers in front of them. The same symbols as those on the wardrobe in their bedroom graced the sides and front. Jonah introduced Mr. Walker.

At first, Lina thought the man ugly with his bony, clean-shaven face, thick pale hair waving to his shoulders, and eyes so light gray they looked almost silver. But she soon saw the intelligence gleaming in those eyes, the obvious strength in his thin frame, and changed her mind. He had an air of gentle competence that made her like him right away.

She welcomed him.

He gave Lina a quick look, then his gaze slid away.

Lina walked over and touched the satiny finish of the chest of drawers with a reverent hand. "You are a master with wood."

"I'll take this one back." Mr. Walker had a rich voice at odds with his appearance. "Plane off the Indian designs. Can do that to the wardrobe as well."

"No!" Lina held up her hand as if to stop him. "They're beautiful and unique pieces."

Mr. Walker gave her a shy smile.

"Koko was an important part of Jonah's life." Lina traced a triangle with her finger. "She was Adam's mother. I'd be honored to use furniture you made for her."

Mr. Walker glanced directly at her, approval in his eyes.

"Someday when Adam has his own home, the furniture will go with him." Lina laughed, lightening the mood. "You'll have to make us new ones then."

He bobbed his head. "I can do that."

"Besides, Mr. Walker, I'm delighted to have a convenient place for my things. I'll be able to put away the trunk."

"I'll haul it up to the loft," Jonah promised. "It will be out of the way there, and you can still use it for storage."

"Now, Mr. Walker, dinner is ready," Lina said. "There's more than enough for you to join us. I won't hear of you saying no."

"Call me Gid, ma'am. And I'd be honored to partake of a meal with you."

Charmed by his courtly manner that was so at odds with her idea of a hermit, Lina smiled and gestured toward the pump. "You can wash up. You'll find soap and a clean towel there, Mr...Gid."

"Yes'm."

Lina turned and went inside.

Adam looked up from his toys.

"You hungry?" she said to him. "It's time to eat."

He smiled at her. "Mmmma."

She picked him up and kissed both his cheeks, then placed him in the high chair and pushed it against the table. She brought a damp cloth over and washed his face and hands, a task that made him scrunch his face, but he allowed her to clean him. Then she tied a fresh towel around his neck.

The combination of minestrone and fresh baked bread sent enticing smells through the room, and when the men walked in, Lina saw Mr. Walker sniff the air in anticipation.

They ate in silence, and Lina enjoyed the obvious appreciation the man showed her cooking.

When Gid slowed to butter his second piece of bread, he spoke. "Did you bring any books with you, ma'am?"

"Lina," she corrected. "Just my Bible, I'm afraid. I don't have any books of my own. I previously worked as a nanny and was lucky in that my employers had a vast library. They allowed me to read when I wasn't with the boys. So I had no need to buy any.

Gid tried to hide his disappointment.

"But my friend Trudy—another mail-order bride—brought boxes of books with her. She married Seth Flanigan."

His silver eyes lit up. "Does she live nearby?"

Lina looked at her husband for the answer.

Jonah shook his head and described the way to the Flanigans.

When Gid learned he'd first have to go through the town to reach the Flanigan home, he shook his head.

"How about this, Gid?" Lina offered. "I'll ask Trudy to lend me some books for you. If I make the request this Sunday, she can have them on the next Sunday. She'd probably be glad to lend you a whole box. You can trade it out for another when you've finished with the first one."

"That's a mighty big request, ma'am."

Lina suppressed a smile of amusement. She didn't want the man to think she was laughing at him. "Trudy arrived with a whole household of furnishings, much of which is stored in crates in the barn. Seth complains—in a good-natured way—about not having space for the animals. I'm sure they'd be glad to have one less box."

"Well," Gid drawled. "Since I'd be doing them a favor, then, yes, I'll take those books."

The man has a sense of humor after all. "Good. That's settled. Why don't you come to dinner on that day?"

His shy smile rewarded her efforts. "A whole box of books and your cooking would be riches, indeed. That's mighty kind of you, Mrs...ah, Lina."

She beamed at him. "I'll make a special Italian meal for you."

"I'd like that just fine."

"Are there any books in particular you enjoy?"

"I like almost all books, but I'm most taken with philosophers from Cicero to Ralph Waldo Emerson and Henry David Thoreau. I'm rereading *Walden* now."

"Why, one of the women at the bridal agency was reading us that book! We'd only gotten halfway through, though, before I left for Sweetwater Springs."

Lina almost impulsively asked Gid if he was looking for a wife but then stopped. *Elegant Darcy, a high society lady, wouldn't choose to marry a poor hermit who lived in the woods. Too bad,* Lina mused. *If it weren't for their different stations in life, they'd be perfect for each other.*

Chapter Eighteen

Early Sunday morning, as the dawn brightened to day, Lina put the finishing touches to her attire, pinning the artificial red peony to the breast of her wedding gown, which was now her best dress. She'd soaked the hem in lye and, with a lot of scrubbing on the washboard, the dirt had come out. Once dry, she'd hung the dress in the wardrobe with a little lace bag of rose sachet pinned to the neck to scent the material. She'd made sure to keep the garment on the far end of the wardrobe, so Jonah's clothes wouldn't end up smelling of roses. Hopefully, the seat of the Dunn's wagon would be clean, and she wouldn't arrive at the church with smudges on her white skirt.

Lina looked at herself in her small hand mirror, angling it to see the back of her head to make sure she'd correctly centered her braided bun but couldn't tell. She wondered if she dared put a long mirror on her list of what she wanted, then shrugged off the thought. *A big mirror is a desire, not a need. A wagon is a need.*

She picked up her reticule containing a handkerchief and two letters—one for Heather and one for her family. Addie said there would be a time after the service to drop off the letters at the depot. She mentioned that she'd probably have mail of her own to go out to her family in Philadelphia.

Lina walked into the main room where Jonah was sitting at

the table with Adam on his lap, playing with the soldiers and the sheep.

The two gave her their identical small smiles.

"Mmmm," Adam said.

"Mmmm, indeed," his father agreed in a teasing voice.

Last night, she'd requested Jonah shave off his whiskers, and she'd trimmed a couple of inches from his hair, so the length was just above his shoulders. And with his mouth and firm chin exposed, her husband was a handsome man who made her heartbeat speed up just by looking at him.

Jonah set Adam on his feet, stood, and walked over to her. He touched her peony pin. "Very pretty. You ready to go?"

"Let me get my hat." But she lingered a few seconds, looking into his eyes.

He smiled at her. "Better take your shawl. I'll tuck it in my saddlebag. It's a fine day, and the almanac predicts we'll have sunshine for the next week. But in Montana, anything can change, and it's best to be prepared."

Lina reached over for her hat, set it on her head, and tied the red ribbons at an angle under her chin—the jauntiness at odds with her mood. She handed the shawl to Jonah, then pressed a hand to her stomach. "I'm nervous."

He tilted his head, looking puzzled.

"A new town. People I don't know. A Protestant church. What if I do something wrong?"

He dropped an arm around her waist in a sideways hug and squeezed. "Guess I feel the same, even if it isn't a new town for me."

Lina leaned into him, enjoying the first spontaneous gesture of close affection she'd received from him. She liked the feel of his arm around her—how the embrace, as simple as it was, made her feel less tense.

"From what I remember of the service, everyone sort of moves together. So if they stand, we stand."

"I can manage that." She rose on tiptoe to kiss his smooth cheek. "We'd best be going if we're to meet the Dunns on time."

"You smell good." A flush darkened his skin, and he stooped to pick up Adam and carry him out the door.

Outside, Jonah's horse, Scout, was tied to the rail. Jonah set Adam into the saddle.

The boy let out a chortle, the first laugh Lina had ever heard from him. But the child's delight in sitting on the horse didn't ease Lina's apprehension at the sight. Adam was so little and the horse so large. If the child fell, he could seriously hurt himself. "He's surely not riding all by himself?"

Jonah looked surprised. "Of course he is."

"But he's so small."

"Adam's been riding with Koko and me since he could sit, and the last few months by himself."

Lina wanted to refuse, but she had no experience with children and horses, so she reluctantly acquiesced. But just in case, she resolved to stay right by Adam's side and watch him like a mother hawk.

ॐ

A man has no call to act so cowardly about attending church. But even thinking the words didn't make Jonah's legs move any faster. Of course, to justify his slow pace, he had the excuse of his son on the horse and his wife in a long skirt marching alongside the child.

This area was tame compared to the forests untouched by the hand of man. Early on, his pa had chosen to preserve the beauty of the woods as much as possible, leaving most trees intact, instead of cutting a broad swath through the forest. Some stumps poked up through the ground. The deadfall was dragged away and chopped up, instead of being left to rot into sawdust.

The way between the Barrett and Dunn homes had once been open and well used. He remembered the two families often sharing Sunday dinners. Or the womenfolk would ride back and forth to visit. Harrison Dunn and his hands helped with the Barrett's harvest, and his pa had lent his aid during the Dunn's roundup and cattle branding.

For a year or so before his mother's death, Jonah had been allowed to ride to the Dunns on his own. Often when his chores were done, he escaped to spend time with the cowboys, watching them work and listening to their tales. He'd eat some of Mrs. Pendell's desserts and play with little Tyler.

But since that time, the brush had encroached on the path. Saplings grew on what had once been beaten dirt. Bushes and clumps of ferns hid small animals. Wildflowers bloomed. Hearing the chirp of a bird, Jonah couldn't help feeling glad Lina could see some of the beauty of the land he loved.

He glanced back over his shoulder. But instead of looking around at her surroundings, his wife kept a hand on Adam's knee, except when she had to drop back because the path became too narrow. At those times, she watched the boy with an anxious expression on her face. Although he wished Lina would ease her protectiveness, he couldn't fault her devotion his son.

Closer to the Dunn's ranch, the trees thickened. Neither Jonah nor his father had logged this far away from the house. He tried to pick the widest path and winced as Lina's footsteps crunched through dead leaves and twigs. His wife wouldn't make a stealthy hunter.

They came to a fallen log about knee-high blocking the trail. The trees grew thick on both sides, and there was no way around with the horse.

"Oh, no! What will we do?" Lina asked.

Jonah gave her a smile of reassurance. "We'll go over it."

Holding the reins with one hand, he stepped over the knee-high log and held out his free hand to her.

Lina gave Adam an anxious glance.

"It's just for a minute. He'll be all right."

She placed her hand in his.

"Climb up," he encouraged.

Lina gathered her skirt in one hand, stepped up onto the log, and balanced.

Instead of just holding her hand while she climbed down, on

an impulse, Jonah moved closer, slid an arm around her waist, and swung her down.

Lina let out a gasp, dropped her skirt, and grabbed his shoulders, her brown eyes sparkling.

"There, see." He kept his hold on her, and they stood still for a moment, looking into each other's eyes. She smelled of roses, enticing him to lower his head and touch his lips to hers in a sweet kiss of exploration.

His wife moved closer. Her lips were soft and full. Her breasts pressed against his chest.

Until Lina, Jonah had never embraced a woman wearing a corset. He remembered one on display in the mercantile—a frilly garment of lace and ribbons. But the stiffness he felt under his arm made him imagine removing Lina's dress and seeing her in her corset and undergarments, and then undoing those…

The horse shook his head, pulling on the reins and breaking the special moment.

He couldn't resist giving her another quick kiss before pulling away. "Hold these." Jonah gave her the reins, stepped over the log and lifted Adam from the horse. "I'll trade you." He handed her the child and took back the reins. "You go on. I'll backtrack and get enough distance so Scout can jump the log. I'll catch up."

Lina gave him a quick nod of understanding, then her gaze slid away. Color bloomed in her cheeks. She dropped a kiss on Adam's forehead and continued along the trail.

Jonah watched her go, seeing the sway of her small bustle, which made his imagination take off again. He backed Scout until the trail widened, and he could turn the horse. He swung into the saddle and cantered down the trail far enough until he could change directions again and head for the log.

The gelding liked to jump, and Scout sailed over the obstacle with plenty of room to spare.

In a minute, Jonah caught up with his wife. Her glance of admiration made an unusual feeling of pride fill his chest. He dismounted, took Adam from her, and set the boy back in the saddle. The trail had widened. Judging from the chop and saw marks on some of the stumps, the Dunns must use this area of the forest for gathering their wood.

Jonah shortened the lead on the reins and walked near Scout's head on the opposite side of the horse from Lina. He was close enough to glance across the gelding at her, and from time to time, they exchanged looks that spoke of a heightened awareness of each other and a promise for the future.

Once through the trees, the grassland opened up. They had only a few hundred yards to walk to reach the road. In the distance, he spotted a wagon driven by Addie with Mrs. Pendell beside her. Several men rode horses on either side. He recognized Harrison Dunn and the foreman, Habakkuk Pendell, but he didn't know the ranch hands.

The two groups came together, and the riders reined in their horses. Addie pulled up, calling greetings and introducing the men to Lina and Jonah.

Tyler wasn't part of the group, and Jonah wondered if the young man had left early to escort a certain lady to church.

Mr. Dunn urged his mount closer. "Morning, Mrs. Barrett. Hello, little sheep." He leaned down and extended a hand to Jonah. "Good morning. Glad you're going to church with us, son. My wife was mighty pleased that you and that pretty bride of yours paid us a visit."

"It was about time, wasn't it, sir?"

The man made a scoffing noise. "You're a man now. Call me Harris. And my wife's Addie."

Although it seemed strange to address the friends of his parents by their first names, Jonah couldn't refuse the warmth coming from the couple. "I appreciate you taking my wife up like this, Harris. Means a lot to her."

Harris shot him a wise look but didn't say anything.

But Jonah caught the message. *This trip is for me as well.* Being sponsored by the Dunns could only help smooth his way back into the community.

Hopefully, it will be enough.

Chapter Nineteen

The closer they came to Sweetwater Springs, the more nervous Lina became about going to church. When they arrived at the outskirts of town, Addie and Mrs. Pendell stopped their conversation to wave greetings at anyone they knew, and Adam, sitting on her lap, stared around in curiosity.

Lina hadn't seen much of the town through the torrent of rain on the day she'd arrived. Today, with the sun shining and the dirt street dry, her new home held more appeal.

But to a woman reared in a crowded neighborhood where, during a stroll down the streets, you'd hear a dozen conversations in Italian with some English words thrown in, smell garlic and tomatoes, and move out of the way of children playing boisterous games, Sweetwater Springs seemed almost...empty and too quiet. Of course, family groups, couples, and individuals all headed in the same direction—to a white-frame building with a steeple rising into the bright blue sky.

Addie pulled up the wagon in front of a large wooden livery stable and set the brake. The men reined in next to her and dismounted.

A man stepped from the open livery door. He had pale green eyes in a thin face and a crooked nose. "You're early, Mrs.

Dunn," he commented and jerked his head to one side. "I'll park your wagon to the left of the stable."

"Thanks, Mr. Taylor," Mrs. Dunn said, handing him the reins and accepting his aid in climbing down.

Jonah looped Scout's reins over the hitching rail and walked over to Lina, reaching up for Adam. He settled the boy into one arm and helped her step down. Once her feet were on the ground, he raised his hand for Mrs. Pendell to help her off the wagon.

With laughter in her eyes, the housekeeper accepted his support.

Harrison gave a stable boy his reins and walked around the wagon, extending an elbow to his wife. The other men secured their mounts at the horse rail and set out for the church.

Addie took Harrison's arm, and the two strolled down the street, exchanging greetings with the parents of a large family, children trailing in their wake like ducklings.

Jonah set Adam on the ground, retaining the boy's hand. With a wink and a ghost of a smile, he mimicked Mr. Dunn, holding out his free arm to Lina.

Her anxiety bolstered by the secret communication, she slipped a hand around her husband's arm, and they walked after the Dunns. Lina was careful to hold the hem of her white skirt above the dusty street, but low enough to provide lady-like coverage of her ankles.

For a few minutes, the novel feeling of parading up the street with her very own family filled her with joy. Then they passed a couple—she, short and heavy-set with a stuffed bird on her enormous hat and he, tall and balding, with a red nose—and Lina caught the disapproving frown the woman directed at Jonah and the man's unfriendly stare at her. In that instant, her good spirits deflated.

Lina was closest to them and forced herself to give the two a polite smile instead of the glare she wanted to bestow on them.

"Disgraceful," the woman huffed. She spotted Adam and her close-set eyes narrowed.

Anger flamed within her, and Lina did her best to tamp it down. *No yelling in Italian for the whole town to hear.* She increased her stride to pick up their pace as much as possible with a toddler anchoring them. *This is what Jonah had warned me about in his letter.* She reminded herself that not everyone was like those two.

Jonah didn't seem to notice the couple. He was leaning toward his son, obviously scrutinizing the toy Adam held up to him.

The woman muttered something else.

But they'd passed beyond earshot, and Lina could only hear the critical tone and not the actual words. A good thing, because if the woman had said one unkind thing about Adam, Lina would have whirled on her and raked her nails across her face.

Since Jonah hadn't seen or heard the woman, Lina resolved to keep the unpleasant interlude to herself. No sense in causing him more pain. She took a deep breath to calm her anger.

Addie glanced back over her shoulder and gave them an encouraging look.

As they neared the church, the curious stares of the townsfolk made Lina uncomfortable, but she forced herself to smile at each person who met her gaze. Slanting a glance at her husband, Lina saw him clenching his jaw. She nudged him with her shoulder. "You look like the grim reaper," she chided in a soft voice. "Try to appear friendly."

"I don't feel very friendly."

She didn't know whether to laugh or commiserate over their similar feelings. "Someday, many of these people will be friends in truth. But today we lay down the foundations of those future relationships."

His jaw relaxed, and he met her gaze. "I married a wise woman."

"Even if I twisted your arm to get you here?"

"My arm? You dang near twisted my whole body." The corners of his lips turned up.

"Jonah! Talking like that on a Sunday," Lina scolded, but she couldn't keep the amusement out of her voice.

From the opposite side of the street, Tyler Dunn, with a buxom young woman on his arm, met up with his parents. After the two couples exchanged greetings, he led her over to Jonah and Lina and performed the introductions, obviously proud to be her escort. His love was called Laura. Lina didn't catch her last name.

"Pleased to meet you," Lina said with a polite smile.

"Mornin', miss," Jonah murmured.

Adam held up his sheep. "Ba."

When she heard Jonah's name, Laura stiffened and gave them both a frosty look, even though her words of welcome sounded perfectly polite.

From his angle, Tyler couldn't see Laura's expression, and Lina suspected the woman's true personality might be lost on him. *His parents are right to be concerned.*

They all moved toward the church, although Laura slowed her steps so she and Tyler wouldn't be part of their group, and then pulled him aside to chat with another couple.

Reverend Norton stood near the door, greeting people as they entered. When he saw Lina, his eyes lit up, softening his austere expression.

The welcome on the minister's face partially eased Lina's annoyance about her last two encounters.

"Ah, the Barrett family. What a blessing to see you all in church on this beautiful Sunday."

Jonah nodded. "Thank you, Reverend."

Trudy rushed up to them, practically dragging Seth by the arm. "I was afraid we'd be late," she gasped out. "One of the horses picked up a stone in his hoof, and we had to stop to get it out before he went lame." She held out a hand to Lina and pulled her close to kiss her cheek. "My dear friend, you don't know how happy I am to see you here." Trudy stepped back and surveyed Jonah with a bold teasing stare. "Why Jonah Barrett, don't you look handsome without your beard."

"Hey," Seth protested, amusement in his voice.

Trudy pretended to ignore him, focusing on Jonah. "I will

take credit in your transformation." Her eyes full of mirth met Lina's.

Lina joined in, remembering Trudy's suggestion about Jonah's beard in her original letter.

Wearing a wide grin, Seth buffeted Jonah's shoulder. "We certainly have turned respectable, haven't we?"

Jonah's smile was wry. "Might have a ways to go still." He picked up Adam.

The church bell in the tower rang, summoning the faithful to worship and setting a clanging echo in Lina's stomach.

Reverend Norton turned and went into the building.

Trudy and Seth led the way inside. At least from her wedding ceremony, Lina knew what to expect, although the Madonna was no longer on the plain white cloth covering the altar. Instead, five vases full of different kind of bouquets covered the surface, and she wondered if several families had contributed blooms from their gardens.

Lina passed by folks who stared at her in curiosity. Some of them glared derisively at Adam. Her stomach tightened. Her fingers wanted to clench, but they relaxed when she also saw welcome on other faces, which somewhat helped her discomfort.

Trudy chose a pew in the middle of the room and motioned for Seth to go in first. She followed her husband, and Lina sat, relieved to be out of view from the stares, with Jonah next to her, Adam on his lap. He clutched his sheep, and she hoped having a toy in church wasn't breaking any Protestant rule.

Addie and Harrison took a seat on Jonah's other side, filling their pew.

A very pregnant woman in a rose-pink flowing dress took a seat at the piano and began to play a passionate piece of elaborate music, which ushered the rest of the congregation into the church.

Trudy leaned close. "Bach," she whispered. "Very well played."

Familiar with the piece from her years as a nanny, Lina nodded. Mrs. Hensley had often practiced the piano in the afternoon. She would also play for her husband and friends in the evening, while the boys listened from the upstairs landing.

The unexpectedness of such beautiful music in this frontier town did much to smooth Lina's ruffled feathers about the earlier encounters and for having to attend a church outside her faith. Throughout the rest of the service, she found the whole experience interesting and actually easier to follow than a Catholic mass. She enjoyed the singing of hymns, the Bible readings, and the wisdom in Reverend Norton's sermon—even if she never quite relaxed.

Adam was well behaved, although sometimes he traded parents, moving from Jonah's lap to hers and back again. At a lull, the boy said clearly, "Ba."

A few women chuckled, but the woman with the bird hat, sitting across the aisle, glowered.

Lina gave her an uncompromising stare right back.

The woman sniffed, lifted her chin, and faced the altar.

Lina cringed inside. The hostility toward her son shocked her. Adam was just an innocent baby.

Later, when Reverend Norton pronounced the final blessing, Lina's first response was relief for having survived the service without making any mistakes. She glanced at Jonah.

The melancholy look was back on his face.

She wondered what he was thinking and wished she could touch him to provide comfort.

Moments later, they filed out of the building and into the late morning sunshine. Seth, Harrison, and Jonah, who still held Adam, were pulled into conversations with some men. And Trudy, Addie, and Lina stood together with Reverend Norton discussing the service.

The pretty piano player came up to them and gave them a friendly smile. Her big blue eyes sized up Lina and Trudy with patent interest. A tiny pink hat, snugged onto the blond curls pinned into a loose chignon, matched the color of her dress. The stylish flowing gown she wore failed to disguise her advanced pregnancy. A tall, attractive man with high cheekbones and a slightly aquiline nose trailed behind her.

Reverend Norton turned slightly and addressed the woman. "Mrs. Thompson, it's good to see you. Are you feeling better?"

Mrs. Thompson gave the minister a rueful smile and touched her extended stomach. "I'm sorry for my absence, Reverend Norton. This little one caused me difficulty for a while. I was ill for weeks. But all is well now, and I insisted Mr. Thompson drive us into town for church. However, I don't think I'll make another service until after the baby is born."

"Mrs. Toffels brought word about your delicate condition. Mrs. Norton, and I have prayed for your health and that of the child."

Mrs. Thompson's luminous smile changed her prettiness into stunning beauty. "Thank you, Reverend Norton. The babe and I are doing fine now. Although I'm quite impatient for his or her arrival."

"Of course you are." He gestured to Trudy and Lina. "Speaking of arrivals, I don't believe you have met our newcomers to Sweetwater Springs. "Mrs. Seth Flanigan and Mrs. Jonah Barrett."

Mrs. Thompson laughed gaily and extended her gloved hand to Lina. "The mail-order brides. I'm so delighted to meet you." She squeezed Lina's hand before taking Trudy's. "Our cowboys kept me informed of the town gossip. I was dying of boredom and confined to the sofa. Whenever one of our men rode into town, I insisted he gather information so I wouldn't feel out of touch with the community. Good men that they are, they made trips to the mercantile, the train depot, and the carpenter shop. They also stopped to chat with folks on the street. Poor dears. Why, I believe they've talked more in the last few months than in the previous five years combined."

Lina couldn't help the giggle that escaped.

Once Reverend Norton saw the conversation take hold between the women, he excused himself and moved on to other parishioners.

"I have a marvelous idea." Mrs. Thompson's eyes danced. "I'll hold a tea party for you two as a welcome to Sweetwater Springs." She glanced at Mrs. Dunn. "Don't you think that's a marvelous idea, Addie?"

Before Addie could respond, Mr. Thompson sent his wife a stern look. "*After* the babe has arrived, and you're back on your feet."

"Oh, Wyatt!" She wrinkled her pert nose at her husband. "Very well." Mrs. Thompson pretended to pout and then perked up. "Then I'll be able to show off the baby to all of you. Shall we say...July 20th?" She raised her brows coquettishly at her husband.

"Later. August 10th," Mr. Thompson said, obviously suppressing a smile. "Just in case the baby comes late."

She rolled her eyes at him and patted her stomach. "Don't even *suggest* this child be late." She glanced at Lina in an obvious appeal for sympathy. "I'm already as big as a horse, and Dr. Cameron still thinks I have three more weeks to go."

Lina couldn't help a pang of envy. Soon Mrs. Thompson would be holding a newborn in her arms. How she longed to do the same.

Mrs. Thompson grasped Lina's arm. "Do you like the idea of a tea party, Mrs. Barrett?" She released Lina and fluttered a hand at Trudy. "And you, Mrs. Flanigan? Please say yes."

Trudy laughed. "Of course, Mrs. Thompson."

This time, Trudy was the recipient of the nose wrinkle. "Oh, call me Alicia. I just *know* we're all going to be good friends. And my husband is Wyatt."

Addie placed a hand on Lina's arm. "I'll drive you to the Thompsons, so don't worry about how you'll get there."

Lina glanced at Trudy, saw her friend's nod of agreement, and said, "We'll be there."

"Wonderful." Alicia clapped her hands. "Shall we say 2:00?"

Lina and Trudy nodded.

"A party will give me something to look forward to after the long confinement." Alicia waved over a stout older woman.

"This is our dear Mrs. Toffels, the finest housekeeper around."

Addie laughed. "I'll have to disagree," she teased. "I have Mrs. Pendell, who's the finest housekeeper in the west."

"We'll have a tie," Alicia said vivaciously. She quickly told Mrs. Toffels about the party.

"Just what you need." The woman nodded in approval. "Planning the party will keep you from fretting about the birth."

Alicia lifted her chin, and Lina glimpsed a flash of apprehension in her blue eyes before the look vanished.

No matter how desired the babe, childbirth is still something every woman fears.

"We'll decide the most important thing about the party right now," Alicia said in a blithe tone. "What is your favorite cake, Lina? Trudy? I can vouch for Mrs. Toffels' coconut or chocolate. But her others are almost as flavorful."

"Coconut," Trudy suggested.

"Chocolate," Lina said at the same time.

Mrs. Toffels beamed at them with good-natured humor. "We'll have both then."

The minister's wife came up to them. "Dear Mrs. Thompson, I have missed your playing in church. I'm so glad you could be here today."

"This is the only chance I have to play the piano, so I love doing it." Alicia made a pretend pout. "I'm afraid you'll have to do without me for a few weeks."

"Well, the congregation will just have to make do with me." Mrs. Norton kept a straight face, although she spoke in a teasing tone. "Unfortunately, just basic hymns."

Alicia's hands fluttered. "Singing hymns is the best part of church! Although don't tell Reverend Norton I said so."

The skin around Mrs. Norton's eyes crinkled when she smiled. "Sometimes, I think so too. Although *not*, of course, when my husband is preaching."

They all laughed.

"Mrs. Norton. I'm giving a tea party for our new brides on August 10th at 2:00 pm. Do say you'll come."

Before she could respond, an older sharp-faced woman walked by, her hand tucked around her husband's arm. He was stooped and thin and seemed to lean against her arm.

"Mrs. Murphy," Alicia trilled. "I'm having a tea party for our new brides on August 10th. I'd so love for you to be there."

Mrs. Murphy glanced at Trudy and gave her a ghost of a smile. "Good day, Mrs. Thompson. Mr. Thompson. Thank you kindly for the invitation. But I don't like to leave my husband for that long."

"Nonsense," Mr. Murphy said in a soft southern drawl. His smile lifted the folds of his face. "There's no need to hover over me. You go enjoy yourself with the ladies. I'll be just fine on my own."

Indecision in her eyes, the woman glanced back and forth between Alicia and her husband; the loose skin under her chin quivered.

Alicia placed a hand on Mrs. Murphy's arm. "No need to give me an answer now. Why don't you determine the state of Mr. Murphy's health that morning and come if you are comfortable."

Mrs. Murphy's face relaxed, and she nodded. "If it's all the same to you, I'll do that, then, Mrs. Thompson."

Trudy gestured to Lina. "Mrs. Murphy, this is my friend, Mrs. Jonah Barrett.

"Oh, yes. The one you bought my chickens for."

Lina gave the woman a polite smile. "Adam has enjoyed chasing them. So far, though, they've managed to evade him."

The woman frowned. "You'd best break him of that habit right away, Mrs. Barrett. It will put them off their laying."

The chickens are too young yet, and it does me good to see Adam playing and enjoying himself. But Lina didn't voice her thoughts out loud. Instead, she inclined her head in acquiescence.

The Murphys moved on and another couple approached the group.

Lina recognized the woman who'd made the unpleasant remark and her back stiffened. She sent a quick glance around to make sure her husband and son were out of earshot, then girded herself for battle.

"The Cobbs own the mercantile," Trudy said in an undertone. "They aren't the most congenial people."

Alicia's smile at the Cobbs was the same pleasant one she'd given everyone else. "Mrs. Cobb, I'd like you to attend a tea party I'm holding for our new brides in August." She gestured to Trudy and Lina.

Mrs. Cobb eyed Lina, a critical look in her narrow-set brown eyes. She opened her mouth to say something, looked at Wyatt, standing protectively behind his wife, and closed her mouth. The shopkeeper shook her head. "I can't leave the store."

"Of course you can." Alicia gave Mr. Cobb a charming smile. "You will hold down the fort quite admirably, won't you, Mr. Cobb?" Her big blue eyes appealed.

He cleared his throat. "You go ahead, Hortense, and accept the invitation. I'll manage without you for a few hours."

Alicia rewarded him with an approving glance. "Thank you, Mr. Cobb. Now I'll just go spread the word about the party. Oh, there's Mrs. Cameron. Let me go ask her." She flitted away.

The Cobbs hurried off in the direction of the mercantile.

Wyatt stared after Alicia, a tender look on his face, before turning to them. "Well, ladies, as you can see, my wife is a force of nature when she wants to be. I predict every woman in the vicinity of Sweetwater Springs will be at her tea party to welcome you two, and you'll all have a wonderful time, even with such disparate elements such as ah, Mrs. Murphy and Mrs. Cobb in attendance."

Trudy laughed. "Your wife does everything with so much charm."

"She's like sunshine," Lina said in admiration, watching the elderly couple talking to Alicia brighten in her presence.

"And very talented," Trudy added. "I so enjoyed her piano playing in church today. That Bach cantata was marvelous."

Wyatt's gray eyes twinkled, and he held one finger to the side of his nose. "Not a word to her, ladies. But I do believe there will be music at your tea party. I've ordered a piano for Alicia to celebrate the birth of our child. It should arrive in three weeks. It's a surprise."

"Oh," Lina said on a delighted breath. "What a special gift." *How very romantic!*

Trudy pulled a face of pretend dismay. "I'm envious. My piano is still in a crate in our barn."

He grinned, his teeth white in his tanned face. "I'd better get Alicia back home to rest. If my wife has her way, she'll talk to everyone who attended church and a few more as well. Next thing I know, she'll be wandering into Hardy's Saloon just to say hello." He touched his hat to them and headed after his wife with the air of an amiable sheepdog about to herd his charge in his desired direction.

Lina stared after them. "What a lovely couple."

"I'm quite captivated by them both," Trudy agreed.

They looked at each other and simultaneously reached out to clasp hands.

"I'm so glad we came here to live," Trudy said, her eyes bright.

Lina looked past Trudy to see her husband following two steps behind Adam, who was toddling his way through the people. "So am I."

Jonah looked up and met her gaze. The way his eyes lingered on her mouth made her remember the kisses of this morning.

So am I, Lina repeated to herself.

That night after Adam had been tucked into bed, Jonah sat on the porch holding hands with Lina and watching the fat sinking sun shoot rays of orange, pink, and gold across the sky. The chickens perched on the porch rail. Jonah reminded himself to take them into the barn before he and Lina went to sleep, but for now, he was feeling too lazy to move.

Beside him, Lina chattered about the day and the tea party.

The friendly welcome she'd received this morning seemed to have eased her concerns about attending a Protestant church. And she went on to describe in detail every encounter she'd had.

Jonah only half listened, sensing Lina didn't need a response. But he liked the sound of her voice, how she sometimes threw an Italian word into the conversation.

He and Koko had often sat here in the evening. But they'd watched the sun set in comfortable silence, appreciating the respite from the day's tasks. Until now, he hadn't realized how much the language difference between them had affected their communication. They'd learned some basics of each other's language, communicated through facial expressions or gestures, growing more fluent with time. But they'd never talked about the larger world outside Sweetwater Springs, nor discussed deeper issues. The love they felt was known to each other but never spoken of.

With a tinge of regret, Jonah thought, *I should have found a way.*

Being with Lina was different. She was vibrant and spoke her mind—almost too much for his comfort. He was conscious of the energy that had simmered between them ever since he'd kissed her earlier today.

Their kiss from this morning had lingered in his mind, making his concentration on the sermon difficult. He wanted to kiss her again, but he was supposed to wait a month to approach her for marital intimacy. *But what if she's ready?*

We haven't been married by Father Fredrick yet. Will that still matter to her?

He tried to figure out ways to find out the answer and started with bringing her hand to his mouth and kissing the back. He lowered their arms to his lap and lightly stroked the skin of her wrist.

Her breathing quickened.

Definitely a start.

"I envied Alicia being pregnant, near her time." She cast a flirtatious look at him from under her eyelashes. "Why, just think, our children could be close enough in age to be friends."

Like a bucket of ice water poured over him, her suggestion caught Jonah's complete attention and chilled any thoughts of seduction. He sat up straight and turned to face her. "No."

"No?" Lina's forehead wrinkled in puzzlement. "You don't think our children will be friends?"

With a sick feeling in his gut, Jonah realized he could not go forward with intimacy, with creating babies. He'd come to care for Lina and didn't want to lose her. "No more babies. Adam is enough."

She tilted her head in puzzlement. "What do you mean, 'Adam is enough?'"

"You told me you loved him like your own child." Constriction wrapped around his chest like a rope.

"I do," Lina protested, pulling her hand away.

"So why do you need more children?"

"I've always wanted children," she said in a patient tone. "And because I love Adam, I want him to have sisters and brothers. I missed knowing Adam as a newborn. I want to hold a baby of my own in my arms. *Babies* of my own."

"No." Panic tied his tongue in a knot.

"Jonah, I don't understand. You love being Adam's father, I know you do. I see how close you are to him. Why don't you want more?" She inhaled a ragged breath. Sudden tears stood in her eyes. "Is it because you don't love me like you did Koko?"

The tension constricting his chest choked his neck. All he could do was shake his head.

Lina stared at him, her hands slack in her lap. "You couldn't have always felt this way. Koko was carrying your second child." She gave a sharp inhale. "Oh!" Her body stilled. The silence stretched as she waited for him to speak.

Finally, the bands around his chest loosened enough for him to talk. "I don't want to risk losing you too, Lina. I can't bear going through that again."

"So, you do care about me?"

"You've become...*important* to Adam...to me."

Disappointment flickered across her face. "I understand," she said softly, reaching for his hand and squeezing.

Her gentle touch was almost his undoing. Tears burned in his eyes, and he blinked them back. "I'd better put the chickens up."

"Jonah, wait, please. Mrs. Dunn said you didn't have Dr. Cameron here for Koko's confinement. Why not?"

"We'd planned to go to her tribe. We did that with Adam— had the herbal woman deliver him. She had an easy birth, and we didn't expect differently for the second one. We'd intended to leave in a few days. I was plowing in the fields when her pains started weeks earlier than we expected. Being the stoic woman she was, Koko didn't ring the bell to summon me."

"I'd never be so brave," Lina murmured with a shake of her head.

"By the time I came in for supper, her labor was too far advanced. When I tried to leave to fetch Dr. Cameron, she wouldn't let me go." He shook his head, trying to dislodge the horror of the memory, but the recollection remained in stark detail. "Koko was a fighter, but the baby was breech. When I finally got her out, she'd…already died. Our daughter was so perfect. She looked just like Adam when he was born, except tinier."

"My heart breaks just thinking of your precious little one."

"And Koko kept bleeding." Jonah dropped his face in his hands. "So much blood. I was helpless to stop the flow. Her life drained away, and I couldn't save her." Despite his best efforts at control, a sob snuck out.

"Oh, Jonah." Lina slipped her arms around him and pulled him close.

He leaned into her, breathing in the scent of rose and Lina, half-ashamed of showing his emotion and half-relieved by the expression of his feelings. Sharing with her eased something that had been tight inside him since Koko's death. No, if he was honest with himself, since his ma's death.

For a long time they sat huddled together, and Jonah let the pain ooze out of him. Neither of them spoke, but Lina kept rubbing his back—soothing circles that brought him comfort.

The dusk deepened. Finally, Jonah pulled away and wiped an arm across his eyes.

"Where are they buried?"

He gestured to the forest. "Koko had a favorite spot—a circular clearing surrounded by trees. I've marked her grave with a cross. I placed our daughter in her arms. Jessabelle was her name. We planned to call her Jess."

"You show me where they lie, and I'll plant some flowers there for them both," Lina promised.

He pictured their grave—stark except for the wooden cross he'd made. "I'd like that."

She took his hand. "Now, I have some things to say about babies."

Lina's determined tone brought some levity into his heavy heart. "I'm sure you do."

"I've had a talk with both Mrs. Norton and Mrs. Dunn about the deaths of mothers and babies in childbirth out here. They've both assured me that since Dr. Cameron's been practicing in Sweetwater Springs, very few women have died."

"But it still happens," he pointed out.

"But Jonah, *life* still happens. I could fall off a wagon tomorrow and die. We all will die. But I don't want to die without having *lived*. And for me that means children—a big loving family like the one I had."

Dread churned in his gut, but he waited for her to finish.

"My grandmother had nine children, who in turn gave her fifty-eight grandchildren and seventeen great-grandchildren, although my cousin Margaret was due around now, so it might be eighteen. *None* of my aunts, sisters, and cousins have died in childbirth. Not *a single one*. We come from sturdy Italian peasant stock." She chuckled. "Although Nonna claims it's the red sauce that keeps us all healthy."

"I thought it was the minestrone."

Lina let out a hearty laugh. "Probably both." She bumped his arm with her shoulder. "I'm willing to compromise. I've always wanted six children. That's what we have in our family. But I'll settle for four."

Four! He shook his head. "I don't think I could survive *four* pregnancies."

"Two, then. But no less. And if I have two boys, I want to keep going until we have a girl. I want a daughter, too."

"What if we have ten sons?" The very idea made his mind want to bolt like a runaway horse.

"Then we'll need a bigger house." She shook a finger at him. "And the minute my pains come, you are to race for the doctor."

"And leave you alone?" He couldn't help the shudder that ran through his body.

She raised her chin. "I'll manage until you return with the doctor."

Jonah raised a weary hand. "Lina, you are like quicksilver. I'm like..." He searched for an analogy.

"A rock," she suggested in a dry tone.

He pulled up a corner of his mouth. "Close. Maybe I'm like earth?"

She leaned over and pressed a kiss on his lips. "What matters to me is that you *will* think it over."

"I will." Knowing how his mind worked, Jonah added, "Might take me a couple of days."

She flashed him a quick smile. "Shall we sit here three days hence and discuss the matter again?"

Three years is more what he had in mind. But the decision had to be faced. He wasn't sure she'd stay if he said no, and they'd best know one way or the other.

Could I bear for Lina to leave? For Adam to lose her? The thought made his heart ache. "Three days it is."

Chapter Twenty

Three days later, Jonah returned from a trip to town, his arms filled with paper-wrapped parcels and the sacks of flour and corn meal Lina had requested. He set the supplies on the table, slid his hand inside his shirt, and pulled out a letter, waving it at her. "From your friend Heather."

"Oh, thank goodness!" Lina clapped her hands together. "I've been dying to know what's been happening with her." Smiling, she took the envelope from him.

"Go on." Jonah gestured to the bedroom, his expression indulgent. "I'll watch Adam while you read in privacy."

Lina pressed the envelope to her chest. "Oh, thank you." She rose on tiptoe to kiss his cheek, then hurried to the bedroom, closing the door behind her to block Adam's chatter. The boy had lately become quite gregarious. Sitting on the bed, she carefully opened the envelope, still warm from Jonah's body, slid out the sheet of paper, and began to read.

Dearest Lina,

Your letter reached me on a day when I needed to feel your spirit. Thank you for always seeming to know when I need you. Although my initial plans did not pan out, I cannot complain too much. I have three jobs. Yes, it is true. I work for Dr. Handerhoosen in the mornings, Berta May in her quaint little sewing shop, and then Mr. Lichtenstein's mercantile in the afternoons. I am earning my way on my own!

Even though I have not forgotten Hayden, there is another handsome cowboy named Roady who is courting me. At least I think he is. He has not made his intentions known but has taken me for a buggy ride out to the prairie and has been keeping me company quite a bit. Morgan approves and seems to be pushing him my way. I do like Roady. It is hard not to. He is quite handsome, has a winning smile, and has the happiest constitution I have ever known. Whenever I start to feel sad about Hayden, I remind myself that things could be much worse.

Before I run out of time—Roady is taking me to a concert in the park soon—I need to tell you about Evie. I have been to her and Chance's home. It is so cozy. She has done a lovely job of settling in. When you see the two of them together, you would think they have known each other for years, instead of barely over a month. I pray that same happiness comes to you and also to me. I don't really know what advice to give you about Mr. Barrett and his son, except I have confidence that you are the medicine they need. Just be yourself and all will be well.

I am sorry to cut this letter short but the kindly woman who lets me a room just knocked on my door to tell me Roady has arrived to pick me up.

Please tell Trudy hello for me. I miss you both terribly. I am so happy you have her shoulder to lean on.

Write soon!

Love,

Heather

Postscript-I have had one letter from Sally. My dearest little Melba is still among us, but Sally fears it will not be long before she flies away home to heaven. Please keep her and my mother and family in your prayers. I know your prayers carry much weight. I love you and think of you often.

Lina read the letter through quickly, then again slowly. At some point, she thought she heard voices in the other room, but, absorbed in her letter, she didn't pay much attention.

When she finished, Lina tapped the paper in her lap. While she was glad Heather seemed somewhat interested in another man, she obviously hadn't gotten over Hayden. Lina could understand how Heather's plucky personality and capacity for hard work would have her trying to make the best of the situation. *This letter is entirely too cheerful, but I sense there is more going on with her.* Lina wished she knew what her friend was really feeling. This letter hadn't eased her concern about Heather one bit. *When I next write, I'll have to chide her about not being completely honest with her feelings.*

"Lina!" Jonah's voice from the other room held a sharp note she'd never heard before.

Adam! Her heart thumping, she dropped the letter and leaped to her feet, throwing open the door, only to see her son in the arms of an Indian girl. Instinctively, she moved toward them, only to gasp in fear at the sight of a stern Indian man.

"No need to worry," Jonah said, the tightness of his tone belying his assuring words. "This is Koko's brother Mingan and sister Sokanon. Will you show them your Italian hospitality?"

Put on her mettle, Lina stiffened her spine. "Of course." She forced a smile and stepped forward, holding out a hand to Mingan since he was nearer, hoping the gesture was an acceptable way to greet him. "Welcome. Have you come to visit Adam? I'm sure he's grown since last you saw him."

The Indian stared at her from solemn black eyes in a craggy, brown face framed by two long braids. He touched her hand with his fingers before lowering his arm to his side.

Jonah translated her words, but as he didn't say as much as she had, Lina wondered if he'd told them everything she'd said. *Maybe he doesn't know all the words.*

The man gestured at the girl and spoke some more.

She was about fifteen or sixteen, pretty with an oval face and brown eyes. Her dark hair flowed lose down her back. The man and the young woman wore fringed and beaded buckskin clothes, although the man's tunic came down over leggings to the hip, and the girl's hem ended at mid-calf.

With a thunderstruck expression, Jonah shook his head. He stepped in front of the girl, laid a hand on her shoulder, and spoke softly to her.

Sokanon swallowed. Her gaze slid to Lina and away before she nodded.

Mingan's expression darkened, and he barked out some incomprehensible sentences.

At the strident tone, Lina's stomach tightened.

Jonah answered, sometimes pausing to find a word, then continuing, his tone calm. Then his mouth quirked, and he spoke again.

Mingan narrowed his eyes, then let out a bark of laughter.

Jonah's shoulders relaxed.

Lina exhaled in relief. "Jonah, may I know what is going on here?"

He glanced at her, a wry smile pulling at his mouth. "Koko's family has been worried about Adam—who would take care of him. So they sent Sokanon to be my wife."

"Be your wife?" Lina said faintly. "Did you tell them you already have a wife?"

"Right now I did. And I told Mingan I couldn't afford two wives."

Not wanting to offend, Lina pressed her lips together to hold in a laugh.

"I think Sokanon's relieved not to have to leave the tribe and live in the white man's world."

"*Oh Signore, such a twist.* Lina waved to the table. "I'm sure they're hungry. Please offer them a meal. Good thing I have plenty of minestrone."

Crisis averted.

At least, she hoped so.

❦

Jonah had never admired his wife as much as he did now. After her initial shock, Lina hadn't batted an eye about her unexpected guests. Instead, she talked to her visitors as she dished out ladles of soup—as if they could understand every word.

When Lina sat in her chair, she looked from Mingan to

Sokanon. "I'll say grace now." She looked expectantly at Jonah, obviously waiting for him to translate.

He closed his eyes and bowed his head. They followed his lead.

Lina recited the prayer in Italian.

After hearing it for so many days, Jonah was becoming familiar with the cadence of the words. Soon, he'd be able to join in.

Once the prayer was over, Lina dipped her spoon into the soup, lifted it halfway to her mouth, and paused. "This is *minestrone. Minestrone*," she repeated.

Guessing what his wife wanted, Jonah repeated the word, nodding and smiling in a way that would give the two Indians permission to say the Italian word as well.

To his surprise, Sokanon was the first to make the attempt, getting the sounds correct but missing the rhythm of the syllables.

Lina grinned at the girl. "Yes, very well done." She gave a pleased bob of her head and spooned soup into her mouth.

Sokanon returned the smile, then sent her brother a challenging glance. "Min-stron-eé," she said.

He scowled, but Jonah could tell Mingan wasn't really displeased, and he managed a mangled version of the word.

"Excellent," Lina beamed and clapped.

Not to be undone, Adam smacked his chubby hands together.

When did he learn that? Jonah realized the boy had probably seen Lina make the gesture every time he did something to please her.

Mingan scooped his first spoonful and raised the utensil, warily eying the noodle trailing over the side. But after he tasted the soup, his expression changed to approval.

Once they started eating, Jonah watched everyone relax. Maybe there really was magic in the minestrone like Lina's nonna claimed. Mingan and Sokanon had bowl after bowl and slice after slice of bread spread with huckleberry jam.

Very little conversation occurred between them. But Koko's siblings both watched Adam as if memorizing his every expression and movement. Thank goodness, they hadn't arrived a few weeks ago, when both father and child were thin and wan. Mingan would have seen how much he struggled in managing life with Adam and insisted Sokanon stay, or worse, suggest Adam live with them. Perhaps out of desperation, Jonah would have accepted her as a wife. He could only imagine the scandalized reactions of the townsfolk if he had done so—not only taken another squaw to wife, but such a young one...

But now, both he and Adam had filled out and were obviously well taken care of. Instead of the withdrawn, clinging child he'd been, his son obviously enjoyed being the center of attention, engaging everyone with eye contact and making sounds that came closer and closer to real words.

After supper, while Lina washed and dried the dishes, Sokanon sat on the floor with Adam, playing with his toys.

Jonah watched them for a few minutes, feeling a bittersweet feeling of kinship. Sokanon didn't look at all like Koko except around the mouth. They had the same smile. His wife had more closely resembled a feminine version of Mingan.

Sokanon brought out a hide doll, with real hair fastened to the head and beads for eyes and a mouth. The doll's dress was similar to the one the girl wore with fringe on the hem and sleeves and a row of red beads across the front. "Koko made it for Sokanon when she was small." Jonah explained for Lina. "Even if it's not a toy for a boy child, she wants him to have it. And—" his voice hitched, and he swallowed hard "—maybe to share it with his sister someday."

Jonah and Mingan engaged in stilted but warm-spirited conversation about Koko's family—their father had sprained his ankle, although now he could move two-legged; their other sister was expecting a baby; the scarcity of game, so the tribe was about to move to another hunting ground. If Jonah and Adam came to visit, he'd need to head toward the painted mountain to find them. He was welcome to bring his new wife, and perhaps she would teach the women the secret of her minestrone.

At that wry comment from Mingan, Jonah laughed out loud.

Obviously encouraged, his brother-in-law began to tease him about an Indian wife being better able to please him, than a white one who wore so many clothes and had to be pampered. Jonah had to suppress an image of Lina in bed with him, being all too able to please him.

His wife turned from putting the bowls on a shelf and raised an eyebrow.

He only repeated Mingan's comment about teaching the women to make her soup.

Her eyes sparkling, Lina looked at Mingan. "I'll send spices and some noodles with Sokanon."

Scooting on his knees, Adam wheeled his wagon, the doll riding inside, toward Mingan.

The man picked up his nephew, perched him on his knee, and began to talk to him.

His son's eyes tracked his uncle's mouth.

I think Adam remembers the language. Mingan had told the boy this story before, and Koko had translated what Jonah hadn't understood. He looked to Lina. "He's telling Adam a story of a boy fostered by a bear. One day, he saw his people when they camped in the area where they'd lost him. He returned to the tribe with sacred and magical presents."

Jonah remembered Koko's animal skins in the loft and climbed up to retrieve them. After she'd finished working the hides, they were soft and supple. She'd left them stacked one on top of each other. He rolled up two and took them with him.

He walked over to Sokanon and laid the roll at her feet. He looked at Lina. "The Blackfoot believe a woman's job is to butcher the game and work the skins. The more she has, the more value she holds. Koko took pride in these. I want her sister to have some."

"That's lovely, Jonah."

The girl's happy smile reminded him of Koko, and he had to turn away.

The hour grew late, and Adam's eyelids drooped. Lina took him to get ready for bed.

Excusing himself, Jonah followed her into the bedroom. "I'll let them have the furs to sleep on in the main room. But I should sleep here with you. Our situation would look strange if I didn't."

Color rose in Lina's cheeks. "Of course. Shall we try putting Adam in the trundle bed? He's quite a restless sleeper."

Without him, we won't have a barrier, he wanted to warn her. "Go ahead. I'll let you get ready first."

Jonah brought out the sleeping furs and spread them in front of the fireplace. The two visitors had also brought their own fur bedrolls.

He left them settling down in the main room by the glow of the moonlight and carried the lamp into the bedroom.

Lina was already tucked into bed, the light blanket they used in the summer instead of the bearskin pulled up to her chin.

Jonah blew out the light, shed his clothes, donned his nightshirt, and got into bed with her. At first, each of them lay stiffly next to each other. Night sounds drifted through the partially opened window—the soft hoot of an owl, the distant mournful howl of a wolf.

The darkness pressed on them, and he was very aware of Lina's warm body beside him, clad only in a nightgown. More than anything, Jonah wanted to take her in his arms and run his hands over her curves.

Lina shifted and then spoke. "We were supposed to sit on the porch tonight and have that discussion."

"Come here." He slid an arm under her shoulders and pulled her to his side. Holding her, feeling the softness of her flesh, Jonah realized how much she tempted his resolve. *How can I live with her as husband and wife and resist my attraction?* The image of his dying wife, their stillborn baby girl, still tormented him.

Jonah ran a hand over her hair, tangling his fingers in the long curls that felt springy beneath his palm. He nearly groaned aloud with male need. For a moment, he remembered Koko's hair falling like silk over her naked body. He rolled over, gathered Lina in his arms and kissed her, banishing all memories of Koko from his mind.

Lina's breathing quickened, and she ran her hand over his nightshirt.

Consummating their marriage vows would be so easy. To make her his in every way. He ached to do so. *But, not yet—if ever.* He struggled with the fear of losing her to the brutal ravages of childbirth.

Lina gently pulled away and laid her head on his shoulder, her hand tracing circles on his chest, as if she couldn't get enough of the way he felt. "Father Fredrick is in town this Sunday," she whispered, her warm breath tickling his cheek. "I hope you don't mind waiting a little longer."

His thoughts at war with his needs, Jonah pulled her close. *Four more days, and I still haven't made a decision.*

❧

The next day, after Mingan and Sokanon had ridden off, dried herbs and pasta noodles in their pouches, Lina sat on the porch darning Jonah's socks and watching Adam chase the chickens around the yard. He'd become sturdier on his feet, and it looked like the pullets would soon be in danger of losing their tails. Eventually, she'd have to put a stop to his game. But not yet. She enjoyed seeing him play and have fun far too much.

Adam pointed. "Hor."

Lina looked up the road to see a man on horseback riding toward them. Her stomach clenched. The rider was too far away to make out his features. She didn't know whether to feel excited or afraid about their first visitor since Koko's family.

Jonah was planting in the field, and she shaded her eyes against the glare of the sun to see if he'd noticed the rider.

Her husband was bent over his task, so she moved to pick up Adam, who protested at being taken away from the chickens. Holding his stiff little body, she hurried to the corner of the porch and rang the dinner bell.

Jonah straightened and looked her way.

Waving her arm in a big circle, Lina signaled for him to join her. Since she'd rarely rang the bell—he always seemed to know when meals were ready—he moved at a trot toward the house, reaching her side just as the man pulled up his roan horse in front of them.

With dismay, Lina saw the black armband the man wore on his shirtsleeve and put a hand to her chest to cover her suddenly beating heart. *Who has died?* She looked up at Jonah in consternation and held Adam tighter.

His brows had drawn together. "You're one of Thompson's cowboys."

The man removed his hat. His thin face was pale, his blue eyes red-rimmed. "Mr. Thompson..." He swallowed, and his Adam's apple moved up and down. "Mr. Thompson has sent his hands out to bring word of sad news."

Mr. Thompson? Lina thought of the tall, handsome man whom they'd met at church. Of his pretty charming wife. *Alicia.* She knew with a sudden clench of her gut. *Please God, no! Not Alicia. The baby!*

She set Adam on the ground so he could toddle off and slipped her hand into Jonah's, leaning into him for comfort.

The man met her eyes. "Mrs. Thompson died two days ago."

Jonah stiffened and passed a hand over his face.

Lina's body froze. She could barely form words to ask the question. "In childbirth?"

"Yes'm."

Tears welled up, and she tilted up her chin to keep them from falling. But they dripped out anyway and raced down her cheeks.

"And the babe?" Jonah's voice sounded hoarse with grief.

"She lives. She's named Christine Alicia. Dr. Cameron says she's healthy."

"*Grazie a dio il bambina e'salva.*" Not until the cowboy gave her a puzzled look did Lina realize she'd spoken in Italian. "Thank God the child is alive," she repeated in English.

"Yes, ma'am. Mr. Thompson bids you attend the burial tomorrow at 1:00. We will be holding the service at the ranch. Mrs. Thompson will be laid to rest there, not at the cemetery in town."

"We will come." Jonah's voice still sounded raw.

Lina held up her hand in a pleading gesture. "Please give Mr. Thompson our deepest condolences."

"Yes'm, I'll do so."

"Will you come inside?" She waved toward the house. "Have something to eat or drink?"

"No, ma'am. But I'll water my horse." He gathered up the reins. "I have to head to the Dunns' next."

Jonah glanced at the cowboy and squared his shoulders. "Will you tell the Dunns we will meet them at the regular place, so they can drive Lina and my boy to the funeral? We've no wagon."

"Yes, sir, I will."

Jonah pointed. "There's a shortcut to the Dunns. Come, I'll show you where it starts. Using it will cut an hour from your ride."

"Thank you, sir."

Lina couldn't hold back a wave of grief. Crying, she rushed into the house and then into the bedroom, yanking open the top drawer of the bureau. She grabbed for a stack of handkerchiefs and scattered dried rose petals on the floor. Judging from the wave of feelings welling up in her, one wasn't going to be enough. She blew her nose into the scented linen square and carried the rest outside, walking to the edge of the yard. Her tears didn't stop flowing.

Jonah returned from showing the cowboy the way to the Dunns, his expression tight. Without a word, he took her in his arms and held her.

"I knew her for ten minutes, Jonah." Lina's tears turned to sobs. "Only ten minutes. Yet I feel like I've just lost a dear friend. Oh, poor, poor Mr. Thompson. I could tell they were so suited...so happy together. I can't imagine what he's going through."

"I can," Jonah said in a soft voice. "All too well."

Those words made her weep for her husband, for he certainly knew Wyatt Thompson's agony. She suspected that hearing of

Alicia's death had ripped the scab off that painful wound. But he was a man, and men didn't cry. So she cried for him.

He kissed her forehead and held her until her tears ceased.

Lina pulled away enough to blow her nose, then laid her head back on his shoulder, grateful for his strong arms holding her close. In the past when she grieved, she did so alone. In a family who all mourned for her brother Luigi after he took his life, sharing feelings only triggered emotional reactions in others, especially her mother. "Thank you."

"For what?" Jonah sounded surprised. He eased back to look at her.

"Just this. Holding me. Letting me cry. Not telling me I'm ridiculous to be so upset when I didn't really even know her."

"I'd just met her, and I'm sad too. She was a woman with the talent of making others care for her. Perhaps because she cared for them."

She lifted her head to stare at him in question.

"Mrs. Thompson stopped to talk to me before she went over to your group. Actually, she stopped to admire *Adam*. Told me what a beautiful child he was…" His voice broke.

"What a lovely gift she gave you—acceptance of Adam. What you've wanted most."

Jonah gazed down at her, his green eyes full of pain. "Mrs. Thompson said she hoped that she would have a child half as lovely."

Tears brimmed again, but she blinked them back. "I'm sure she did. Her baby must be beautiful."

"We'll see Christine Alicia tomorrow for ourselves."

"I hope they'll let me hold her. I'll probably have to vie with every woman in town." She thought of Mrs. Murphy and Mrs. Cobb. "Well, almost every woman."

Jonah let out a long breath. "I suppose we'd best get back to work. That field won't plant itself."

"Yes." Lina tried to smile at her husband, to reassure him that she was all right.

Jonah dropped a kiss on her forehead and turned to walk back to the field.

The feel of his lips lingered on her skin, and Lina touched the spot before slowly lowering her hand. She made sure Adam was in sight, sitting in the dirt and digging with a spoon she'd given him earlier.

With a heavy sigh, Lina wandered up to the porch. Her hands trembling, she picked up her wooden darning egg that was stuffed into Jonah's sock and took a seat on the bench. She set one crooked stitch, then another, before giving up and lowering her hands to her lap.

This isn't right!

She had socks to darn, dinner to cook. Jonah had fields to till. All the usual tasks of life.

But doing everyday chores seems so wrong!

The whole world should stop and mourn the loss of Alicia Thompson—a woman who created sunshine wherever she went.

What will this do to Jonah?

Lina's tears welled up again and spilled over—for the loss of a friendship, for a baby without a mother and a husband without his wife...and most of all, for her Jonah, who was so full of painful memories.

Chapter Twenty-One

The next afternoon at the Thompson ranch, on a day filled with sunshine, the whole world seemed to mourn the passing of Alicia Thompson, for no birds sang in the grove of aspens, sheltering the small meadow where she would be laid to rest.

Lina stood between her husband and Trudy in the huge circle of people surrounding the open grave. Looking down at Alicia's wooden casket, she wanted to weep, imagining the beautiful woman inside the polished pine box. *Thank God her baby does not lie in her arms.* She glanced across the grave at a stone-faced Wyatt Thompson, cradling his sleeping daughter, his body frozen in grief, his gray eyes like ice crystals.

Next to him, Mrs. Toffels dabbed at her red eyes with a handkerchief, then blew her nose. Hers wasn't the only handkerchief in sight. Most of the women and many of the men wiped their faces. The air practically vibrated with the sorrow of the gathered mourners.

Lina glanced up at Jonah, holding Adam close to his chest, and his bleak expression made her chest ache. She wondered if he'd buried Koko and Jessabelle all by himself, and concluded he probably had. She couldn't imagine conducting such a painful act alone, denied the comfort of a loving family and friends to support you through such a tragic occasion.

Reverend Norton stood at the head of the grave, his wife at his side. Although he must have read the burial service many times, he often paused, as if controlling his own emotions. He took a shuddering breath and read from Isaiah: "Fear thou not, for I am with thee: be not dismayed; for I am thy God." His voice steadied. "I will strengthen thee; yea, I will help thee; I will uphold thee with the righteousness of my right hand."

The familiar words hit Lina like a blow, and she recalled when last she'd heard them read—at her brother's funeral. She clamped down a moan of pain, remembering the darkness of that time when she was thirteen after her beloved older brother lay dead by his own hand. Her grief for Luigi came rushing back as fresh and raw as if she'd lost him yesterday. She swayed with the effort not to wail. The Sweetwater Springs folk did not wail as her family had done. They were…stoic, though she knew they mourned deeply for the vibrant Alicia.

Jonah tucked a steadying hand under her elbow.

Grateful for his support, she leaned against him.

On her other side, Trudy shot her an anxious glance, lifting her eyebrows in inquiry. "Are you all right?" she whispered.

Lina nodded but knew she was lying to her friend. In addition to her sadness, she felt heavy and disheartened. With Alicia's death, Jonah might very well refuse her the children she longed for. Their marriage would remain sterile. Her husband would continue in his melancholy state. For even though lately, at times his spirits seemed lighter, and he'd made an effort to be among people, her doubts remained. *Has he really changed on the inside? What if he hasn't? What if he's like Luigi, headed for the dark abyss, now that Adam has me for protection and care?*

Despite their age differences, Lina and her brother had been special friends. She'd been closer to him than all her other siblings. She, more than anyone else, had known of Luigi's struggle with his inner demons and often tried to tease and cajole him into better spirits. At times, he improved, and the whole family breathed in relief. Why, the weeks before he killed himself, he'd seemed happier than ever, his emotions steady. The night before he died, he'd laughed and joked with them at dinner as if nothing was wrong. They'd all been so full of joy the evening before he'd ripped apart the fabric of their family.

At Luigi's burial, her mama had wailed out his name. Papa, holding his wife, had wept aloud, tears dripping down his face— the first time she'd ever seen him cry. Nonna and Nonno had leaned into each other like two aging trees buffeted by a wind they could not withstand. But Lina had stood dry-eyed and full of anger, fiercely wanting Luigi alive so she could yell and throw things at him. She wanted to pound on his chest with her fists before collapsing into his arms and feeling the beat of his heart against hers. *Alive!*

It was not to be. The Napolitanos had mended and patched the fabric of their family, but nothing had filled the hole in their hearts left by Luigi.

No matter how much I tried, I couldn't save my brother. And I can't change Jonah either… No matter how much I love him. Her heart cramped at the realization—a pain that felt almost physical. *I was sure I could make him happy, give him children, and bring him back into society. But that might be impossible.*

Slowly, Lina straightened away from his support.

Jonah must choose life himself.

❦

Jonah felt eight years old again, holding his father's hand and standing in front of his mother's grave in the cemetery behind the church. A crowd had bunched around them, although not as many as were here today; the town had grown in the twenty years since his mother's death.

He remembered the bewilderment of a child not understanding the finality of death and the intensity of the emotion of those around him; of not wanting his mother to be in heaven, and most of all, the crushing load of guilt. The baby had killed her—the brother he'd prayed for. And because of those petitions to the Almighty, Jonah believed it was his fault his ma had died.

That night, Pa succumbed to drunkenness for the first time. He'd sat at the table and wept. "It's my fault your mother left us, Jonah. If only I hadn't put that baby inside her!"

As he stood listening to the weeping of Mrs. Toffels and others, realization hit. He inhaled a painful breath. *I have double guilt to bear.* Even though Jonah hadn't gotten drunk after Koko's death, he'd held the same belief as his father. He'd murdered his wife as surely as if he'd put a knife into her. And he hadn't wanted responsibility for the death of another woman, his Lina.

As if I'm the hand of God to have such power.

Jonah glanced down to see teardrops glittering on Lina's eyelashes. He felt the love and compassion in the circle around him. Shared pain. Multiplied, perhaps, but also emotional and—he glanced at Reverend Norton—*spiritual* sustenance his father had denied himself. *And I've done the same.*

Adam made a sound of distress and squirmed to get down. "Shhh, son," he whispered, giving the boy a little jiggle.

Lina reached out her hands. "Let me take him," she whispered.

He gave her the child but not before pressing a kiss to Adam's forehead. *Thank God for my son.* Without him, Jonah would surely have turned into his father. He saw the pit clearly now—the deep dark chasm he'd teetered on the edge of and would have fallen into.

Now, Jonah glanced tenderly at Lina. He'd stepped away from the pit and had married this woman at his side who was doing her best to tug him into the light.

I will try harder to go with her.

Chapter Twenty-Two

After the Dunn's dropped off Lina at the path through the woods which led home, Jonah dismounted and walked beside his wife, while Adam rode Scout. She and the boy were uncharacteristically quiet. Jonah hadn't realized how much he'd become used to Lina's chatter, and her silence made him uneasy. The burial seemed to have affected her as deeply as it had him. Perhaps he was the one who'd have to start talking. *When we get home*, he promised himself.

Halfway to the house, Jonah halted, staring down a game trail that broke off from the main one, struck by an idea.

"What is it?"

"Koko's grave is in that direction about a fifteen minute walk."

Lina's gaze followed the trail. "Would you like to go alone? I can follow the path home." Her smile wavered. "I'll even lead Scout. We'll be fine on our own."

Moved by her offer, Jonah ran a tender finger down her cheek. *My wife has her own brand of courage, rooted in her nurturing heart.* "You can come too. But it's only a game trail, and we'll have to go single file. I'll carry Adam on my shoulders so you don't have to fret about him the whole way."

The corners of her mouth turned up, but the smile didn't change the sad look in her eyes.

He reached for Adam and lifted him off the horse, setting him on his shoulders.

The boy chortled and knocked Jonah's hat askew.

"None of that, now." He took off his hat and held it. "Think you can lead Scout?"

Lina glanced from him to the horse, her face pale. She held out her hand.

"Good girl," he said softly, giving her the reins. "Soon, you'll tell me you're ready to ride."

This time her smile seemed a little wider. "Soon." She gingerly patted Scout's neck.

He moved down the path, careful to keep watch for lower branches, sometimes having to lower Adam from his shoulders, then duck under a tree limb.

In a short time, they came to the clearing where Koko and Jessabelle were buried. The grass sloped up to a gentle hill. The breeze blew through the evergreens, carrying the spicy scent of pine their way and rustling the leaves of the aspen trees at the edge of the clearing and of the old oak spreading thick branches over the grave.

Jonah traded Adam for Scout's reins. Without a word, he unsaddled the gelding and took off the bridle, allowing the horse to graze, and spread the saddle blanket next to the grave. He and Lina took a seat and watched Adam chase after a butterfly, laughing. Unknowingly, he ran over the grave of his mother and baby sister. Jonah imagined Koko's spirit, holding their daughter in her arms and watching their son at play. *She'd approve of Lina,* he thought. *How she's brought joy back into Adam's life. Into mine.*

Lina's gaze followed the boy. "Ever since I arrived here, I've wanted to see him smile." Her eyes became teary. "To see him happy on such a sad day… He's the brightness in a time that's dark."

"Koko's people have a saying… 'What is life?'" Jonah quoted. "'It is the flash of a firefly in the night. It is the breath of a buffalo in the wintertime. It is the little shadow that runs across the grass and loses itself in the sunset.'"

"That's beautiful," Lina murmured. "And so true." The breeze blew curly tendrils loose from her braided bun.

Jonah reached over and gently tugged one corkscrew until it stretched out. "Alicia's death has really hit you." He released the curl and watched it bounce back into place.

"Do you think my reaction is strange?"

He shook his head. "In ten minutes, she forged a friendship with you. I'm sure you've spent years with other female acquaintances and didn't find them nearly so congenial."

"Yes." She let out a long breath. "And I'm sad for Wyatt Thompson. He loved her so. I can't even imagine the pain he must be in." She gave him a steady look. "And I worry for you—that this death has…" She reached over and patted the surface of the grave.

He stared at the cross, struggling to put his emotions into words. "I first saw Koko galloping her horse, laughing, her hair streaming behind her. I was caught by her energy." He smiled, remembering. "I had to fiercely bargain with her father before he allowed us to marry. Luckily for me, the young man she'd been betrothed to as a child had died. She cost me four horses and fifty dollars."

Lina's eyes rounded. "You paid for her?"

He playfully poked her side with his finger. "I paid for *you*, wife."

She rolled her eyes. "My train ticket and the agency fee."

His expression grew solemn. "When she and Jessabelle died…" He held his hands out in front of him. "Lina, I felt their deaths were my fault. I believed that everything I touch dies— my ma because I'd prayed for a brother, Koko and my daughter… I thought I was bad luck, that my parents had named me true."

"Oh, no, Jonah!" Lina set a hand on his knee. "Your mama, Koko…they *wanted* those babies. Participated in making them."

"Today I saw that more clearly. Before yesterday, I'd have said Thompson was the luckiest man around—wealthy, a big ranch, a lovely wife he adored…"

"Death happens to all families," Lina said, averting her gaze.

Hearing the bitterness in her voice made him study her face and see her stricken expression. "Who died in yours?"

"My brother, Luigi, hung himself when I was thirteen." Her voice faltered. "He was my favorite brother—the second oldest child. He always made time for me, sometimes even playing dolls together. But as he grew older, he was not a happy young man. I would see his melancholy and try to make him feel better." She shook her head, twisting her hands in her lap. "Only fleeting good moments, then he'd sink back down."

Jonah put an arm around her.

Lina rested her head against his shoulder and proceeded to tell him the tragic tale of a young man who couldn't find happiness.

Listening to her story, Jonah recognized Luigi's struggle, for he'd often wrestled with dark spirits.

At one point, Lina's voice broke, and she began to cry. Feeling helpless to fix her pain, all Jonah could do was hold her. The tears turned to deep sobs that wracked her whole body, and he tightened his arms around her.

Adam returned to them, his face concerned. He plopped down and patted Lina. "Mmmma."

Gradually, the sobs lessoned, until Lina sniffed and pulled a handkerchief from her sleeve. "Good thing I brought plenty today," she mumbled, sitting up to wipe her face and blow her nose. "I never cried for Luigi." Lina's eyes and nose were red, but she looked beautiful in her vulnerability. "At first, I was too angry."

Sensing she wasn't looking for a response, he brushed aside a curl that had stuck to her wet cheek.

"I feel…" Lina paused, her eyes taking on a faraway look. "I don't know if *better* is the right word. Like something raw and angry that I'd carried for far too long has changed… Comforted? Soothed?" She shook her head. "I don't know. It felt good to talk about him. In our family, we don't because Mama always cries."

Jonah gave her a tender smile. "The first night you were here, you offered to talk about Koko whenever I wanted. That gesture meant a lot to me, and I'm glad I could do so for you as well. I'm sure you have many Luigi stories. You can add them to the ones you'll tell us at supper."

Lina laughed and pressed a kiss to his mouth, then leaned over to hug Adam. "Speaking of our meal. We'd best be going home, or else we'll be eating at midnight!"

The next morning after milking the cow, Jonah carried the half-filled pail of milk to the house. As he walked across the porch, something made him pause in the doorway.

Lina stood at the stove, humming and stirring the ever-present pot of minestrone. She must have started a new batch, for surely they'd scraped the bottom the night Koko's family had visited.

The now-familiar aroma made Jonah's mouth water but also reminded him of the first morning Lina had made the soup. *Cure's heartaches*, her nonna claimed. And she'd been right.

In a few short weeks, Lina had taken an empty house and two hurting men—even if one wasn't yet two—and created a family. In that moment, Jonah knew he'd come home. With a lightness of step, he walked inside.

She turned and smiled. "Ah, just in time. Pour the milk into the glasses, would you?"

"After breakfast, I'm going to make a trip to town."

Wide-eyed, she stared at him. "To town? You just were there. We don't need anything."

Laughter bubbled up inside him. "We need some huckleberry jam," he said with a straight face.

Shaking her head, Lina set down the wooden spoon and walked over to Adam. She picked up the boy. "Whatever is going on with your papa?" Lina addressed her comment to the child as if he knew the answer.

"Paa."

"Yes, your pa. He used to avoid Sweetwater Springs like the plague. Now, counting Sunday, he's gone three times in a week." She shook her head and nuzzled the boy's cheek. "Let's eat something, *carissimo*, and start our day. We'll deal with your papa later."

Jonah watched the by-play in amusement. *Oh, yes, my dear. You certainly will.*

Chapter Twenty-Three

The morning chores were well advanced and Adam was taking a nap, when Lina heard the sound of hoofbeats and the creak of wagon wheels. Puzzled, she checked on the boy, then moved to the doorway.

The horses looked familiar, and Lina saw Jonah was the driver. She gasped, hurried across the porch, and trotted down the stairs.

Jonah set the brake and swung down from the seat, holding the reins.

When she reached him, with a flourish he deposited the reins in her hands. "Your chariot, m'lady."

Her mouth opened and closed like a fish. "Mine?" Hope rose in her heart.

"Yours," he echoed and held out his hand. "Come, climb up."

With a happy laugh, Lina did as he bade her.

Once she was settled on the seat, her husband climbed up beside her. "Well, what do you think?"

"Oh, Jonah!" Tears welled in her eyes. One spilled over.

With one finger, he wiped away the moisture. "You deserve the finest carriage with velvet seats and a team of white horses with plumes on their heads to pull them."

"Don't be silly, *caro marito*." But inside, she thrilled at his romantic words. "How? How?" she stuttered, spreading her free hand to indicate the wagon.

"I talked to Mack Taylor at Thompson's yesterday. He had one he'd bought from a family who'd gone back home to the East. Since he'd gotten a deal, and the wagon was just sitting around the livery taking up space, he let me have it cheap." He paused. "I'm sorry I've been so stubborn about buying one."

Lina stared at him with wide eyes.

"I didn't want you to see people look at me…treat me the way they did. See you lose respect for me. Or worse, have to see the town's judgment fall on you—cause you pain and shame all because you'd married me not knowing what you faced. Instead, I caused you pain. Brought unnecessary turmoil into our marriage."

He watched her expressive eyes as she absorbed what he'd said.

An expression of mischief crossed her face. "As long as you never do so again," she pretended to scold.

Jonah laughed. "Father Fredrick will be here this Sunday," he reminded her. "We'll be able to drive to town ourselves."

"Yes!" Lina let out a happy exhale and cupped his cheek with one hand. "You couldn't have given me anything I'd like better."

Leaning close, he cocked one eyebrow? "Nothing? I seem to recall you wanting babies."

Babies! Her heart leaped with hope. Lina narrowed her eyes at him and lowered her hand. "Don't toy with me, Jonah Barrett!"

With a jerk of his thumb, he gestured to the wagon bed. "Whether injury, illness, or childbirth, we can get to Doc Cameron. No need to suffer out here alone."

Her gaze soft, Lina let out a long sigh.

"I love you, Lina. You've brought sunshine into my life." Jonah pulled her toward him. "We take one baby at a time. I'm willing to try *once*. But only if you promise not to…"

"I won't! I promise." Lina giggled and wiggled her way closer until her mouth was inches from his. "*Ti amo, mio marito.*"

He raised one eyebrow. "Saying…?"

"I love you, my husband," she repeated. "I will *not* leave you and Adam and my newborn *bambino*," Lina said in a firm tone, before pressing her lips to his.

⸙

My dear friends,

Even as I write this, I wonder if any of you still reside at the Mail-Order Brides of the West Agency, or if you've moved on to start your own adventures with your new husbands.

I want you all to know that I have found happiness as a wife to Jonah Barrett and a mother to his little son, Adam, whom I love as if he were my own.

Life in Sweetwater Springs (a quaint town) wasn't quite what I expected, especially since Trudy hadn't warned me about the lack of a Catholic church. In her defense, she didn't know there wasn't one. So, I urge you all to make sure you write to your prospective grooms regarding the specifics of the houses of worship where they reside. In any event, Mr. Barrett and I have settled into a mixture of attending the Protestant church except for the Sundays a traveling priest holds mass.

As you know, my husband was previously married to an Indian woman. Imagine my surprise when her brother showed up one day with a wife for Mr. Barrett! After my husband and I overcame our shock, we had a delightful visit—or at least as delightful as could be given I didn't understand their language. Afterwards, they left, and Mr. Barrett didn't end up with two wives.

But we have had two wedding ceremonies! The first with kindly Reverend Norton and the second with Father Fredrick, a priest who ministers to his Catholic flock once a month, weather permitting.

We have amiable neighbors in the Dunn family, who have a ranch toward the north of us. Mr. Gideon Walker, our nearest neighbor to the south, is a shy man, who lives in the forest and makes the most beautiful furniture—really unique pieces—and is quite the reader. Darcy, you and he share the same tastes in books! If you should decide you want to live a reclusive, simple life with a man you can talk philosophy with, I have the perfect match for you.

I'm blessed to live near a town where I can see Trudy Flanigan every Sunday. She's also driven out to see me on one occasion. Yes, our Trudy is driving a wagon by herself and looking quite the experienced frontier wife. I hope to soon learn to drive the new wagon Mr. Barrett recently bought for me.

There are plenty more eligible gentlemen in Sweetwater Springs, ladies, and I hope to have more of you decide to join Trudy and me in this town where we have found loving husbands and a congenial community.

All the best.

Mrs. Jonah Barrett, nee Lina Napolitano

Sitting on the bed, Lina reread the letter before folding the paper and slipping it into an envelope. Glancing at her son napping in the trundle bed, she rose and went in search of the husband she had come to trust and adore.

THE END

Montana Sky Series

In chronological order:

1882

Beneath Montana's Sky

1886

Mail-Order Brides of the West: Trudy
Mail-Order Brides of the West: Lina
Mail-Order Brides of the West: Darcy

1890s

Wild Montana Sky
Starry Montana Sky
Stormy Montana Sky
Montana Sky Christmas: A Sweetwater Springs Short Story
Collection
Painted Montana Sky: A Sweetwater Springs Novella
Glorious Montana Sky
Sweetwater Springs Christmas: A Montana Sky Short Story
Anthology

Look for future Montana Sky books, novellas, and short stories.

About Debra Holland

New York Times and *USA Today* Bestselling author Debra Holland is a three-time Romance Writers of America® Golden Heart® finalist and one time winner. She is the author of the *Montana Sky Series*, sweet, historical Western romances and *The Gods' Dream Trilogy*, fantasy romance. In February, 2013, Amazon selected her book *Starry Montana Sky* as one of the top 50 Greatest Love Stories.

Debra has written a nonfiction book, *The Essential Guide to Grief and Grieving* from Alpha Books (a subsidiary of Penguin). Sign up for her newsletter and receive a free download of *58 Tips for Getting What You Want From a Difficult Conversation* at her web site: http://drdebraholland.com

Also look for her:
Facebook: https://www.facebook.com/debra.holland.731
Twitter: http://twitter.com/drdebraholland
Blog: http://drdebraholland.blogspot.com

Made in the USA
Charleston, SC
15 December 2014